Echoes in the Hallway

Echoes in the Hallway

Gina Becker

Writer's Showcase
San Jose New York Lincoln Shanghai

Echoes in the Hallway

Writer's Showcase
an imprint of iUniverse.com, Inc.

For information address:
iUniverse.com, Inc.
5220 S 16th, Ste. 200
Lincoln, NE 68512
www.iuniverse.com

ISBN: 0-595-17371-3

Printed in the United States of America

This book is lovingly dedicated to my mother,
Angela Bacuros Barkay

A LETTER FORM THE AUTHOR

Dear Reader:

My maternal grandmother sailed to America from Greece to marry a man who was already in the country. Although my mother tells me that her mom did not leave a young love behind in Greece, I used that premise as a catalyst for this story.

Echoes in the Hallway is a moving story of love lost, and a second generation of chances. Much of my writing time was spent researching World War II, the terrain and customs of Greece, and interviewing my mother, who lived in Greece for two years. I hope you will find as much pleasure in reading it as I found in writing it.

Very Truly Yours,

Gina

Acknowledgements

THANK YOU,

George, for your unconditional love and support.

Mom and Dad, for your inspiration.

Lauren, Andrew, Jason, Christine, George Jr., Jamie, and Sarah,
for allowing me the time to write!

Charlotte and Clare for your valuable editorial help.

1940, Crete, Greece…

Separated by war-torn Greece, and by interfering parents, Nikoli and Diana find their hopes of being together are in vain as they succumb to cultural pressures and marry spouses that have been approved by their parents.

1972, Chicago, Illinois…

More than thirty years later, unusual circumstances bring the children of Nikoli and Diana together, and they find themselves faced with an undeniable attraction towards one another. When Alexis discovers the truth of her mother's past love, she has to decide if she will remain faithful to the memory of her father or if she will follow her heart.

CHAPTER ONE

GREECE, OCTOBER 1940

"Diana, did you hear? We're going to war!" Nikoli said excitedly, his dark eyes shining. To a nineteen-year-old young man, the thought of going to war, and defending his country, was a new and exhilarating proposition. Italy's dictator, Benito Mussolini, had made demands to gain access to the Greek seaports. In response, Metaxas, the leader of Greece had replied *'Oxi'*. No.

"I don't want you to go. I want you to stay here with me! Remember? You said we could get married and have a baby." Seventeen-year-old Diana reminded Nikoli with a pout that he could not resist.

Tenderly, he kissed her jutting lower lip. "I'll come back and build a house for us to live in. Then we can get to work on making a baby."

Melting into his arms as the sea crashed against the rocks below, Nikoli could tell Diana anything and she would believe him. Here, in this magical place where they both were free to love each other, anything seemed possible.

"Promise me you'll be careful. I don't want anything to happen to you."

Still facing each other, holding hands, Nikoli looked into her eyes. "I, Nokoli Agorinos, promise thee, Diana Persephonus, to return to thee. Unharmed, unchanged, and undeniably in love with thee."

Diana's heart burst with love and anguish at his words. "What will I do without you here?" Passion radiated from the very core of her body.

"You will think of what you will do when I return. What *we* will do."

Nikoli was Diana's first love, and as far as she was concerned, he would be her only love.

When Diana had first taken notice of him, Nikoli had been cleaning the fishing nets after a night of working off of his father's boat. Diana had been casually walking along the white, sandy shore of the Mediterranean Sea, the warm, blue water lapping at her bare feet. She had paused to observe as Nikoli diligently checked the fishing nets for defects.

Fishing was a traditional way of life for men of mainland Greece and the surrounding islands. Crete, the southernmost island, was no exception. It was here that Nikoli had learned as a young boy to prepare for a livelihood at sea.

Most of the fishing was done at night with the use of dinghies that carried powerful gas lamps to attract squid and small fry into the nets.

Nikoli couldn't have looked more unattractive than he did at the end of a long night of work. Nor could he have smelled worse. When Nikoli had looked up briefly from his work to push a lock of hair off of his forehead, he caught Diana watching him, and fell in love instantly. From that moment, he knew she was the girl that he wanted to marry.

The early morning sky had been a perfect shade of blue, the sun warm, promising to get warmer yet—a prophetic overview of how the love between Nikoli and Diana would grow to an all-consuming heat.

From that day forward, for the following three months, Diana had come down to the sea at the same time every morning to visit Nikoli, sometimes bringing him a jug of fresh water to quench his thirst. Because Nikoli's work was accomplished at night, he would sleep during the day. Eventually, he and Diana also started meeting in the early evening, as the sun was setting beyond the horizon.

Diana had always been a dreamer. Her mother and father hoped to one day soon marry her off to a wealthy man who could care for her in the way she had become accustomed to. It was a tradition for parents to arrange a marriage, and it was a young person's duty to marry whomever their parents chose. Diana hoped that when the time came she could explain to them that she already knew whom she wanted to marry, and her parents would understand.

The sun was setting now as the two lovers held hands, swearing oaths, promising themselves to each other. Nikoli, handsome son of a fisherman. Diana, beautiful daughter of a small café owner.

"I *will* return. You'll see." He looked so strong, so confident.

"When do you leave?" She asked, not really wanting to know the answer. Wanting it to be "never".

"Tomorrow. In the early morning we set sail for the mainland. It is in the northern territory that we must defend our border," Nikoli explained.

"No. Not tomorrow, that's too soon!" She could feel the emptiness crouching behind the rocks, waiting to devour her.

Nikoli knew he must kiss her and leave. Quickly, before he allowed her to change his mind and run off somewhere and hide. This was his chance to prove his manhood and fight for his country; this beautiful paradise that he felt fortunate to live in.

Crushing Diana's body against his, he kissed her as he never had before, devouring her, so that he would remember her taste always. When he released her she buried her head in his neck, breathing deeply of him.

Nikoli pulled away prepared to leave. "I love you, Diana."

As he walked away from her, the sun, heavy and low, was sinking behind the water. With it sank Diana's heart.

"Nikoli!" The wind carried Diana's anguished cry out to sea.

Isadora and Constantine Persephonus had made a comfortable life for themselves in the tiny fishing village where they lived on the island of Crete. Their two-story home was of medium size and built of white-washed stone. There was a large, open kitchen with an eating area, a living area, bathroom, master bedroom on the first floor and a smaller bedroom on the second floor.

Constantine was the owner of the Café Parthenon, a well-kept and popular meeting place for villagers and visitors alike. Coffee roasting in the open air and brewed to perfection was the first thing you would smell when walking past the Café Parthenon. Lunches and dinners consisted of freshly roasted lamb, seafood, rice, bread, and local wine.

Diana loved working in her father's café. She enjoyed talking with the patrons who would come there for coffee or to dine. Often, they would tell her how much they loved her father and his food, and how beautiful she had grown up to be. Diana worked hard taking orders, serving food. She also helped to prepare the food between breakfast, lunch and dinner. Among other things, her father had taught her how to carefully handle the Philo dough, without tearing the thin delicate sheets, to make baklava and spinach pie.

When Diana walked into her house the night that Nikoli had said goodbye, her mother was sitting at the kitchen table with a letter in her hand.

"*Chriso mou.*" My Golden One, Isadora said, addressing Diana by her pet name.

"Mama, I'm tired. Please, if you don't mind, I would like to go to bed. I don't mean to be disrespectful." Diana's family, like most Greek families, was usually very affectionate and would spend time talking before retiring for the night.

"What is wrong, *poulaki mou*?"

Diana paused, wanting to tell her mother about Nikoli, hoping, or rather wishing, she would understand. However, knowing her mother would *not* understand, Diana said, "Nothing, mama. I'm just tired tonight." She walked over to Isadora and kissed her dutifully on the cheek.

Isadora looked at the letter she was holding in her hand, then at her daughter. Sensing that now was not a good time to speak with Diana about the content of the letter, she gave her daughter an understanding smile. "Good night, dear," she said.

Diana went upstairs to her small bedroom. Walking over to her dresser, she poured water from a clay pitcher into the matching clay bowl, then splashed the tepid liquid onto her face several times. After patting her face dry with a clean white towel, she lay down on her bed and curled up into a ball, trying to ease the aching sense of loss that was knotted up in her stomach.

Looking over at the table that was beside her bed, she noticed the small starfish Nikoli had given her. Picking it up, she held it close to her, pressing the sharp, spiny creature against her bare skin. She felt numb, beyond tears.

Nikoli will not be harmed. He will come back to me and we will do all of the things we talked about. Over and over, she repeated the words silently to herself until she fell asleep.

Constantine Persephonus had heard the talk days ago at the café. Word had traveled swiftly of Mussolini's demands for the Greeks to allow access to mainland Greek seaports. General Metaxas refused, and the resistance groups were active, especially on Crete.

Young men and boys were preparing to go to war to drive the Italians back across the Albanian border.

Closing and locking the door of his café, Constantine headed for home, a few minutes' walk from the café.

His wife greeted him with a smile. "Darling, how was your day?"

"Ah, Isadora, this war is heavy on my mind."

"We are strong people and have often had to fight for our independence." Isadora replied.

"Yes, but this may turn into something even bigger than what we've seen in the past. The Germans are determined to take over all of Europe."

Not wanting to speak of war any longer, Isadora said, "I received a letter from my sister in America. She said that she knows a café owner there who is seeking a wife. Preferably a young, Greek girl."

"Is that so?" Constantine kissed his wife's smooth cheek before sitting down in a chair at the wooden kitchen table. Isadora continued to speak as she prepared a cup of herbal tea for her husband.

"She also said that America is a land filled with opportunity." While waiting for the water to boil, Isadora returned to the table and picked the letter up to look at it again, contemplatively.

"Is that so?" Constantine repeated himself, wondering exactly what his charming wife was building up to. He had learned, over the years, that she was a woman of wisdom. Careful consideration was given to every thought and word. Instead of demanding things, she would use her finesse to present her desires in such a way that Constantine found hard to refuse.

"Is it your wish to travel to America?" Constantine asked, drawing his dark, thick, eyebrows together.

"Well, no. At least, not at this point." She held out the black and white photo that looked as though it had been taken recently. "Look here, Lela has sent a picture of the café owner who is looking for a wife."

Constantine regarded the man in the picture. Standing next to a tree, wearing a dark three-piece suit, he looked to be about 5' 8" tall. Although he wasn't smiling into the camera, his dark eyes betrayed a sense of humor.

"He looks like a kind man. Don't you think?" Isadora was slowly building up to the main purpose of this conversation. She was at the stove again, pouring hot water over the strainer filled with loose tea. She placed the mug of steaming tea in front of Constantine as he critically examined the picture.

"I suppose. It's hard to tell what a person is like from a photograph." Constantine shrugged his shoulders. "So, tell me what it is that you want? Do you want to go to America and be with this café owner instead of staying here with me?" he asked playfully.

"Surely, you are teasing me. My dear, I would never leave you for another man. Who else would care for me and understand me the way that you do?" Isadora asked with all sincerity.

"Then, if you are not leaving me, and you don't want to go to America, what is it?"

"Diana." Isadora said her daughter's name matter-of-factly, assuming Constantine would understand exactly what she meant.

"What about Diana?"

Holding up the picture, she repeated, "Diana?"

Constantine grabbed at his chest, at the real or imagined ache there. "Now *you* are teasing *me!*"

"Think about it. This is our connection to America! What with the war coming, it would be the best thing for Diana to keep her out of harm's way."

Constantine stared at Isadora, speechless. She had been a beauty at the age of 18 when he had married her. Now, at the age of 37, she was still just as beautiful to him, if not more so.

When Constantine's parents had first told him that they had chosen a wife for him to wed, he had been furious. As was the custom then, and still was to this day, he had no choice but to obey his parent's wishes. To his delight and relief, Constantine had found Isadora dark, slender, and desirable. Her eyes were the most unusual shade of green with flecks of gold, and he had felt desperately lost in emotion when he looked into them. It was then that he wondered what she must have thought about him. Compared to her beauty and gracefulness, he had felt ugly and foolish.

Isadora had bore a son who had died at birth, and less than a year later, she gave birth to Diana. Over the years, Constantine had worked hard to provide a good life for his wife and daughter so that they would be proud of him and want for nothing. The love between Isadora and Constantine had grown strong and resilient.

"Isadora," he took her slender hands in his and smoothed his thick, work-worn thumbs over the back of them. "Diana is still a child."

"She will be eighteen soon. I was only eighteen when we were married."

"Still, I would miss her. She is our only child." Constantine persisted.

"All the more reason we should be concerned for her safety and welfare."

"But America is so far away!" Constantine could tell that he was losing this battle.

Isadora kissed his cheek. Ten years her senior, she still found him very attractive.

"My sister is there. She will make sure that Diana adjusts to life there."

Throwing up his hands in defeat, Constantine let out an exasperated sigh. "I can see that you are determined to have your way, no matter how much I contradict you."

"Is that a yes?" She asked hopefully. She would never raise her voice, or demand her way. If Constantine did not agree, she would accept his decision.

"Yes," he agreed quietly. It really was the best for Diana. He and Isadora could join their daughter once he had a better idea of which way this war was really headed. If it became necessary, he would close up his café and start over in America.

"Thank you my dear. You are a wise and loving husband." Isadora threw her arms around Constantine and kissed him deeply on the lips.

"You better not kiss me like than unless you intend to follow through," he warned.

"Maybe I do," Isadora broke away from their embrace, playfully running to their bedroom as Constantine ran after her.

CHAPTER TWO

When Diana awoke the next morning, she was overwhelmed by the returning, aching emptiness. Slowly, the memory of last night came upon her and she remembered the reason for the void she felt inside. The familiar smell of morning coffee percolating on the stove, and fresh bread baking in the oven, reached her bedroom from the kitchen below. Usually a welcome aroma, Diana's stomach churned at the thought of food this morning.

Diana slipped on a clean, white cotton dress, and a pair of brown, strap-on sandals. Pulling her long, thick dark hair into a ponytail, she twisted it and secured it with a seashell clip her father had given to her as a gift. Without her usual liveliness, Diana made her way downstairs.

"Good morning, Diana." Her father was sitting at the kitchen table with her mother. Each of them had a steaming cup of fresh coffee in front of them.

"Papa, why aren't you at work today?" She kissed him on his cheek and sat down at the table to join her parents.

There was an uneasy silence as Isadora looked over at Constantine.

"What is it? What's wrong?" She was panic stricken with the thought that maybe someone had seen her and Nikoli together, and now she was in trouble with her parents.

"Diana, our country is going to be at war, and you will be eighteen soon." Isadora began, haltingly. Looking at her only child, she realized that this was going to be more difficult than she had originally thought.

"Yes, in one more month."

"Your father and I were thinking that it was time you put away your girlish dreams and started thinking about marriage."

Diana perked up slightly. "Yes, I have thought about that too."

Constantine, clearly surprised, asked, "You have?"

"Yes, Nikoli has promised to marry me when he returns from the war." She looked down shyly, her long, dark eyelashes sweeping against her cheek.

"Nikoli?" her mother asked in confusion.

"Oh, mama, he is so handsome. And his father has his own fishing boat and Nikoli helps him every night. I have been going down by the sea every morning to visit him and taking him a jug of drinking water." In her enthusiasm, she had said far too much.

Constantine slapped his open palm down on the table so hard that both Isadora and Diana jumped. "I'll not have any daughter of mine visiting a boy without my permission. Do you understand?" he growled.

Although tears had formed instantaneously in her eyes, Diana dare not cry in front of her father, he would think she was weak. Instead she sat in stony silence.

"Your mother and I have decided to send you to America. There is a man there who is seeking a Greek wife. He owns a café, like me." Although Nikoli was not an arrogant man, this was said with a measure of self-importance.

This isn't happening. Diana thought. *I'm not hearing him correctly.*

Isadora was holding a picture of a man in front of her face. "This is the man that my sister wrote to me about. His name is André Stephanos."

Diana looked at the picture and cried, "Mama, he's too old for me." She didn't care if she was being impertinent. This was a discussion about the rest of her life.

Isadora placed an understanding hand over her daughter's. "Sometimes a good husband does not look like the man of our dreams, and sometimes the man of our dreams is not a good husband, *poulaki mou.*"

"I am not your 'little bird'. You cannot do this to me. I won't let you." Diana's voice was becoming shriller with each word.

"Enough!" Constantine had never heard his daughter use such forceful language with them. How dare she tell them what was allowable.

"There is a war in progress. Greece wants to stay neutral, however we have no choice in the matter but to defend our border. This opportunity from America could not have come at a better time. I intend to book passage on a ship that leaves for America in one month."

"One month? But papa, I'm too young to travel all alone to America. Please, please don't make me go." She would beg if necessary.

"There will be others who are leaving the island. You can travel with them. I will make sure you are safe and comfortable on your journey." The discussion was coming to an abrupt close.

Diana frantically sought her mother's eyes with her own hoping to find comfort there as she had when she was a child. Instead, she found betrayal.

At that moment, in her heart and mind, she had ceased being their daughter. How could they do this to her, the very people who were supposed to protect her and care for her?

Stiffly, she got up from her chair. "May I please be excused." She averted her eyes, looking at the floor.

"Of course," Isadora replied smoothly, before Nikoli could protest.

Diana stepped out into the bright sunlight. A soft, warm breeze caught the strands of her hair that had fallen loose, blowing them around her face as she walked. Reaching the beach, she went over to the spot where Nikoli usually brought his father's boat in. In its stead was a different boat she had noticed on other occasions. It belonged to one of the many older fisherman who also made his living out at sea.

"Good morning, pretty one. Nikoli has gone off to war, surely you must have known?" the old fisherman said in his gravelly voice. He had a snow-white beard and mustache, and overgrown hair that blew around wildly in the breeze beneath his navy blue fisherman's cap.

"Yes, I knew. I was hoping it was all a bad dream and he would be here as usual."

He looked at her with knowing eyes. "Sometimes, all of life seems like a bad dream."

Their eyes locked briefly, with shared pain. "My parents are sending me to America, because of the war. They also say that there is a man there who owns a café and is seeking a Greek wife."

"We are at war. Your parents want the best for you." The man paused to light a cigarette.

"It's not fair. I don't want to go."

"Life is not fair, my young one. You will learn to cope." With the cigarette dangling from his mouth, he picked up his catch and headed for town.

Diana's mind was reeling with plots and schemes as she tried to conquer her torturous thoughts. Maybe she could run away and live in the caves, or on a high mountaintop with the monks. Then, when the war was over and Nikoli had returned home, she could come out of hiding and be with him. Could one really cut off their family ties so completely? She knew she would miss her mother and father if she ran off without telling them. No, running away was not an option.

One month, that was all the time she had to convince her parents to let her stay and marry Nikoli. If she couldn't convince them, then she would have to live with the hope that Nikoli would gain passage to America and find her. Their love was too strong to fall apart just because of a war.

With renewed courage and determination, Diana headed for home.

CHAPTER THREE

Diana's passage to America aboard the *Vulkania* was, for the most part, uneventful. Two long weeks were spent on the ship. Many of the travelers suffered from seasickness. Although Diana wasn't one of them, she felt a pang of empathy, but it was her heart that was sick, not her stomach. Diana spent much of her time alone on the ship's deck, running her hand along the smooth, wooden rail, watching the clouds as they drifted by, and looking out at the seemingly endless ocean. Her mind was filled with thoughts and memories of Nikoli.

Every day, just before lunch, a siren would sound signaling each and every person aboard to report to his or her lifeboat station. This daily drill would prepare them for an emergency at sea. The younger children thought this was a fun game, but the somber faces of the adults told another story. Occasionally, Diana would spot the periscope of a submarine, a silent reminder of the reality of war.

For entertainment, men and women would show off their talent in the dining area by singing and dancing, or playing an instrument. Cigar-smoking men played card games, while the women took turns styling each other's hair, and talking about the big plans they had once they reached America.

Somewhere along the way, Diana had gotten the notion that America was a land of excitement and adventure unlike any she had ever experienced in her homeland. Women were allowed more freedom in America. They had maids to do their housework, and many of the women worked outside of the home. Children were cared for by nannies.

The men and women in America wore exciting clothes that were purchased ready-made from fancy department stores. The streets were paved smooth with cement, and almost everyone owned their own automobile.

By the end of her journey, Diana was actually looking forward to discovering this strange, New World for her herself. She would send a letter to Nikoli, and he would come to join her there, for that was the one thing she was sure of—Nikoli would come looking for her. Once he returned home from the war, he would discover that she had gone to America and come after her.

Every night Diana would dream of Nikoli. Memories of his kisses and the passion they had shared warmed her on the cold fall nights at sea. Diana occupied a small cabin with three other girls her age, and sometimes she would share with them the love she had for Nikoli.

All of the girls were being sent to America for nearly the same reason as Diana.

Their families were in fear for their lives because of the war, and they hoped that their young offspring would find suitable husbands in America who would be able to take care of them and perhaps send money back home to their family members in Greece.

"My parents want me to marry a man who is nearly ten years older than me." Diana said. It was late evening. Diana and the three other girls were lying in their beds talking.

"Oh, that's terrible!" One girl replied into the darkness.

Another voice piped in. "That's not so bad. At least he'll be established. I bet he makes good money,"

"Nikoli will come for me. When he returns from the war and finds I'm gone, he will come to America and look for me."

"What if he doesn't come home?" Yet another voice speculated.

"Don't ever say that again." Diana's voice was tense and clipped, forbidding further conversation.

The room fell silent as everyone pretended to be too tired to talk anymore. Each of them falling asleep, thinking their own private thoughts, dreaming their own dreams.

AMERICA, DECEMBER 1940

At twelve thirty, on a Sunday afternoon in early December of 1940, the ship carrying Diana and two hundred others sailed into the harbor of Ellis Island. On the neighboring Staten Island, the Statue of Liberty, torch held high, was an exciting and imposing first glimpse to America.

The ship buzzed with excitement as those aboard prepared to disembark. Nervously, Diana made her way to the main deck and followed the other passengers off of the platform. The air was much colder than Diana had expected, and she pulled her sweater closer together with one hand, while holding tightly to her suitcase with the other.

Although Diana was detained in immigration for half the day, she passed through without any major complications. Her father had taken great care to ensure that her papers were in order. The fact that her Aunt Lela was already a citizen of the United States and expecting Diana made the transition through immigration a smooth one.

Lela had consistently sent reading material and educational books to Diana and Isadora so that they could learn about America and the English language. Diana was prepared for her trip, and could speak and understand English very well.

After a tearful good-bye to the other girls she had shared her small cabin with, Diana looked at the written instructions her father had given her. The next thing she was supposed to do was take the ferry to the mainland and hail a cab that would take her to the train station.

Once on the mainland, hailing a cab proved slightly more difficult than she had anticipated. Constantine had told her to behave as though she belonged and she would be treated that way. Looking around her at the native New Yorkers, she held up her hand and waved wildly at each approaching taxi cab only to be pushed aside by someone else who was also waiting when the cab pulled up to the curb.

After suffering this dilemma three times, Diana decided she'd had enough. When the fourth cab pulled up beside her, another pedestrian came running over to it. Diana aggressively opened the back door, threw in her one and only suitcase, and hurriedly shut the door.

Glaring out the window at the other would-be passenger, Diana said to the driver, "Train station, please," as the cab made its way into traffic.

Constantine had arranged for Diana to have a private berth on the train so that she would be able to get some rest before arriving in Chicago. The berth was narrow and had a bunk bed on one side, and a tiny closet and desk with a chair on the opposite side.

Noticing a complimentary packet of stationery and pen on the desk, she sat down to write a letter to Nikoli.

If only Nikoli hadn't been away at war she wouldn't be in America. He would have been able to prevent all of this from happening by proving to her father that he was worthy of being a suitable husband for her. It wasn't his fault that he'd had to go and fight for his country. It was his duty.

Diana knew that it was only a matter of time before Nikoli would be able to come for her. He would return safely from the war, find out that she had been sent to America, and then he would gain passage on the next ship sailing out of the Greek seaport. She couldn't live without him, and surely he couldn't live without her.

Eagerly, she picked up the pen and wrote:

> *My dearest Nikoli,*
>
> *I hope that by now you are back from the war. To me the war is a dark and ugly monster that separated me from the one I love, and I hate it! I am now on a train headed for Chicago, where my*

Aunt Lela lives. My parents intend for me to marry a café owner there, but I will not do it. How can I when it is you that I love?

I think about you nearly every waking minute. Oh, Nikoli, come to me as soon as you get this letter. You must save me, save my life! Please, please come to me as soon as possible. I love you, and always will.

Forever yours,
Diana

Tears were falling onto the paper. Hot tears of pain and frustration that seemed infinite. She felt a primitive anguish consume her and, unable to sit up any longer, stepped weakly over to the bed to lay down. Her head fell heavily upon the pillow.

All night long, Diana lay there unmoving. It seemed as though she had lost all sense of time and place. She didn't even bother going to the dining car for supper. Throughout the night, she drifted in and out of a restless slumber, the rocking of the train repeatedly lulling her back to sleep.

The following morning, feeling somewhat renewed emotionally, and hungry, Diana ate breakfast with the other passengers. Tomorrow she would be in Chicago where her aunt would pick her up from the train station.

Returning to her room, Diana wrote a letter to her parents telling them of her journey thus far. Then, she gave the letters addressed to her parents and Nikoli to the train's concierge, paid him for postage, and watched with anxiety as the letters were placed with the other outgoing mail.

It would take at least two weeks for her correspondences to reach Greece. Diana had addressed the letter she had written to Nikoli to his parent's home, hoping that they would forward it to him or give it to him when he returned home from the war. Diana had thought of sending a letter to the army base where he was stationed, but she wasn't sure where that was or if he would receive it there. Once Nikoli received the letter, and responded to it, another month would have passed. The whole process took so long!

An apprehensive, impatient knot formed in the pit of Diana's stomach. She shivered, and wrapped her arms around herself. The only thing left to hold onto was hope.

CHAPTER FOUR

In 1935, the royalist supporters took power and King George II took the throne. Instead of a president, a king was once again ruling Greece.

It was at that time that Diana's Aunt Lela had decided to go to America in search of a better way of life for herself. Her husband, a sailor, had drowned at sea and she was childless. She felt that Greece no longer held any promise for her, and she went in pursuit of a new existence.

Lela had gained employment working as a maid for a wealthy American family. She saw, firsthand, the privileged lives these people led. Lela often hoped that she would meet a wealthy man who could give her all of the wonderful things the people she worked for had.

Once or twice a week, for the past five years since coming to America, Lela had been going to the Café Skyros which was owned and operated by André Stephanos, who had arrived in America with his parents when he was eight years old. Now, at the age of 28, André worked day and night to make a success of his small business. Brightly lit, clean and always boasting a good deal on breakfast 'served anytime', the Café Skyros was always busy.

"What can I get for you today, Miss Lela?" André Stephanos was a handsome, good-natured man. His golden brown eyes held a secret passion, and he always had a witty comment or two on the tip of his tongue. At 5' 8" tall, he was slender and stylishly dressed in a starched white, cotton shirt and pleated, tan trousers. His dark brown, leather shoes were freshly polished to a shine.

"I'll have your famous Greek omelet, wheat toast, and a cup of coffee." Lela didn't need to look at a menu, she knew it by heart.

André wrote out the order on a green slip and hung it on the order wheel, giving it a spin so the cook would see it.

Turning back to Lela, coffeepot in hand, he picked up an empty brown coffee mug. Tossing it up in the air with a spin, he caught it by the handle and set it down in front of her, filling it with the dark, fresh brew.

Next, he made his way down the counter and topped off the mugs of other customers who were also drinking coffee, occasionally asking questions. "Anything I can get for you right now?" or "How's that son of yours doing?"

André loved the customers who came into this restaurant. He was extremely proud of his establishment and enjoyed serving people, and it showed. Those who frequented the place felt as though André were part of the family making him privy to all kinds of information including business decisions and family disputes.

When Lela's food was ready, André garnished the plate with a slice of orange and a sprig of parsley. Setting the steaming plate in front of her, he asked, "So when is that beautiful niece of yours coming in from Greece?"

"I'm picking her up from the train station tomorrow. You didn't forget our agreement?" She raised her eyebrows expectantly.

"No, of course not. And I never go back on my word." André was standing in front of her at the counter and speaking in a low, but firm voice.

"You won't be disappointed," Lela said, taking a bite of her toast.

"I hope not." André smiled, as he studied her briefly. The tinkling of the bell on the front door drew his attention. Picking up his order pad, he left Lela to her meal and greeted the customers who had just come in.

Lela inwardly felt her confidence waver slightly. What if Diana had grown fat and ugly over the years instead of beautiful like her mother had been. Lela had always been envious of Isadora's beauty and of her good fortune in life. It seemed that there was a light around her younger sister that was impenetrable and all good things were bestowed upon her.

Now that the opportunity had presented itself in the form of a war, Lela was going to take some of that good fortune for herself. If Diana had turned out to be half the charming beauty Isadora had been, then André would certainly want her as a wife. And, if that were the case, he would have to allow Lela to live with them in his beautiful home, which was what they had agreed upon. At thirty-nine years of age, Lela had given up any hope of ever marrying again.

Lela had it all neatly planned out in her mind. She would introduce Diana to the drudgery of daily life working at the Johnson's beautiful home. Lela would point out to the young girl that she, too, could enjoy the same comfortable lifestyle, instead of a life of toil, if she could capture the attention of André.

Finishing the last bite of food, Lela left money on the counter to pay for her meal and waved good-bye to André.

CHAPTER FIVE

"Look at you! You're all grown up, and so beautifully too!" Lela hugged Diana tightly. With great relief, she stepped back at arm's length to take a good look at the tall, dark, slender beauty before her. Diana's eyes, like her mother's, were the most beautiful shade of green. They created a striking contrast to her dark hair.

"Aunt Lela, you look wonderful, too. You don't look a day older than when you left Greece." Diana meant this with all sincerity.

"Nonsense! I've been working my fingers to the bone day and night to make ends meet." She held up her dry, overworked hands. Noticing the thin sweater Diana had on, she said, "You'll need a coat. I have an old one you can wear."

"I only brought one suitcase with me. It was all they allowed me to bring. I never had need for more than a sweater back home." Diana indicated the one she was wearing now, which wasn't enough to protect her from the cold December wind.

"I can't wait to see where you live. Is it a big, beautiful house like the ones I saw in the picture books you sent us?" Diana asked anxiously, following her aunt out of the train station and onto the street where Lela went about hailing a cab.

"Well, sort of. I can't afford to live alone, so I live in an upper flat."

Diana had never asked her mother about her aunts living arrangements and was disappointed that she would be staying in a house with strangers living below her. Her parent's home in Greece had been a single-family dwelling.

Picking up on her niece's change in mood, she reassured her. "It's not bad. The other tenants and I stay out of each other's way for the most part."

"Do you go to parties and wear fancy dresses?" She wondered what else was going to be strange and different about this new place.

"Parties? Fancy dresses? Who have you been talking to? Haven't you read a single one of my letters?"

Diana could feel her apprehension growing. "All I know is what my mother told me. She would read your letters and then tell me what was in them."

"I cater fancy dinner parties for the wealthy people I work for. The people who attend them wear the most fabulous clothes. The men as well as the women! I've already arranged for you to work there with me."

"Oh. When do I start?"

"You'll come to work with me tomorrow morning. Mrs. Johnson is expecting me to bring you." Lela said as she settled herself, Diana, and the suitcase in the first cab that pulled up to them.

Diana looked around in amazement at the tall buildings. They were unlike any she had ever seen before. "The buildings look as though they might topple over onto us!"

"You'll get used to it. The city is really being built up. There is so much room for growth and opportunity here." Lela loved Chicago with its clean streets and modern buildings.

"The streets are so smooth. It looks just like the pictures in the books you sent us." Diana was impressed with her new surroundings. There were no dusty, gravel roads here.

"You're English is great," Lela said, pleased that her niece had picked up the language so quickly.

"Mother and I would practice speaking, writing and reading English nearly every night."

Fifteen minutes later, the cab pulled up to a small, brownstone building. It was boxy looking and had four windows facing the street.

Lela paid the cab driver after he set Diana's luggage on the sidewalk. "We're the two upstairs windows." Lela pointed out to Diana who was looking up at the building.

Diana nodded and smiled as she followed Lela inside and up the stairs.

Lela's flat was small, but comfortable and nicely decorated. The living area had a loveseat with a quilted blanket neatly folded across the back. There was an eating area, complete with a round table and two chairs. The kitchenette boasted a range, a refrigerator, and a sink. The one bedroom had a narrow walk-in closet and a chest of drawers, which was placed squarely against the wall next to the twin-sized bed.

"Would you like something to drink? I have Coca-Cola or Vernors." Lela said graciously.

"I've never had either one." Diana said.

"Of course, I forgot." These products were not available in Greece. Lela removed the cap with a bottle opener from the glass bottle of Coca-Cola, and handed it to Diana. Without hesitation, she drank eagerly, directly from the bottle.

"Diana, a lady drinks from a glass, not from a bottle." She went to the cupboard and took out a glass. Gently taking the bottle away from her niece Lela poured half of the bottle of soda into the glass and gave it to Diana.

"This is delicious!" Diana said, as she took demure sips from the glass, trying to impress her aunt.

"That's much better," Lela smiled approvingly at her. "You can put your suitcases in my bedroom for now. I've cleaned out one of my dresser drawers for your use, and you can hang your dresses up in the closet. The love seat is comfortable to sleep on, although your feet might hang over the edge."

For the moment, all thoughts of Nikoli had vanished while Diana unpacked her suitcase. She was even excited about starting work tomorrow at the Johnson's. As with any adventure, everything seemed shiny, new, and hopeful.

In her hometown where she was sure of her identity and place in the world, Diana was thought to be a daring and headstrong girl. In America, she appeared to be a simple-minded optimist. She was ill prepared for the coming events that would change her entire life.

ॐ

The following day, Diana and Lela set out for the Johnson's house. Cold gusts of Chicago wind nipped at their cheeks giving them a rosy glow. Lela had given Diana one of her old winter coats to wear.

"Do you walk to work every day?" Diana asked, disappointed because she thought that her aunt would have an automobile.

"Yes. I'm lucky to have found work so close to home. It only takes me ten minutes to get there." Lela's pace was quick and she walked with long, purposeful strides. Occasionally, she nodded hello to a familiar passerby. Diana struggled to keep up with her aunt.

Ten minutes later, true to her word, Lela led Diana up the long driveway of the Johnson's palatial house. Diana felt a leap of excitement when she set eyes on the beautiful two-story, red brick home. The entire street was lined with similar homes set on spacious lots surrounded with trees.

Diana was headed for the front door, but her aunt laughingly called out to her, "Back door, silly! We never, ever use the front doors. We only polish the brass handles on them."

With a wistful look at the tall, English Oak doors, Diana followed her aunt around to the back of the house.

Once inside, Lela instructed, "Take off your shoes and put these on."

She handed Diana a pair of what appeared to be ballet slippers. She hung Diana's coat beside hers on a hook near the back door and lined their shoes up side by side.

"What's that delicious smell?" Diana asked, following her aunt into the large, well-stocked kitchen. Pots and pans of various sizes hung from a large rack suspended from the ceiling. At the stove, a tall black man with a white apron tied around his ample belly was stirring something in a pot.

"That is the smell of food cooking made by the world's greatest chef. Cooky, I would like you to meet my niece."

Cooky turned around to face the two ladies with the biggest, whitest smile Diana had ever seen. She had never met anyone with skin as dark as his and couldn't help gaping at him.

Lela nudged Diana. "Don't just stand there, say hello!"

Diana quickly recovered and found her manners. "Pleasure to meet you. My name is Diana."

Cooky laughed heartily, his tummy jiggling up and down as he did. "Welcome to America, Diana. In your honor, I've prepared my special hot cereal." He turned to the stove, doled out portions for all three of them and set the bowls on the island counter that had barstools around it. They were in the eating area designated for the staff. The owners of the home never ate in the kitchen where the food was prepared.

Diana sat down and breathed deeply of the aroma of fresh apples, cinnamon and brown sugar mixed in with oatmeal.

The three of them ate and talked. Cooky had many questions for Diana, which she answered politely. Contrary to his size, he was a gentle and kind man and Diana took an immediate liking to him.

Fifteen minutes later, Diana was set to work polishing the wood, of which there was plenty. The furniture and floors were made of wood, and some of the walls had wood paneling. By the end of the day, Diana was exhausted. She had never worked so hard for so long in her life. It was much different than working at her father's café where she could work at a more leisurely pace and take a break when she felt like it.

At the end of the day, Lela and Diana wearily put on their shoes and coats and headed back home. The weather was just as cold as it had been that morning and Diana pulled the coat's collar tighter around her neck.

So far, nothing in America had been as she thought it would be. The air was much colder here, and there wasn't the knowledge that the warm, beautiful ocean was only a walk away. Instead of being a privileged daughter of a business owner, she was being forced to work for wealthy strangers. A pang of homesickness swept over her and she looked at her aunt walking beside her, wondering if she, too, ever missed Greece.

Feeling Diana's eyes on her, Lela glanced over at her niece and smiled. "You did a wonderful job today, Diana. I'm proud of you and I know Mrs. Johnson will be too. You're a good worker."

"Their home is beautiful. It was actually a pleasure to clean such a fine place."

"Yes, it is beautiful. Tomorrow we will polish the brass and silverware."

Diana shrugged indifferently. "Whatever needs to be done, I'll do it."

"That's exactly how I feel about the situation. But maybe one day, you and I will be able to live in a beautiful home too, if we're lucky."

If I'm lucky, Nikoli will come for me soon, and either take me back home to Greece or start a life with me here, Diana hoped inwardly.

CHAPTER SIX

Diana looked at the American money Mrs. Johnson had placed in her hand. Twenty-five dollars to be exact. "Thank you for a wonderful first week of work, Diana."

Mrs. Johnson was slender, tall and blond. In her mid-fifties, she was very well-kept. Her blond hair was swept up on each side and held in place by a decorative comb, and she had make up on—something Diana was not used to seeing.

"Thank you, ma'am." Diana smiled appreciatively at her new employer.

Lela had received her pay as well and was relieved that Mrs. Johnson was so pleased with Diana.

It was a Saturday afternoon. Usually, Lela worked for Mrs. Johnson Monday through Friday. However, if the Johnson's were having guests over on the weekend, as they were that evening, Lela would work from eight in the morning until twelve o'clock noon so that the house would be spotless. Sometime, Mrs. Johnson would ask her to return in the evening and cater the party as well.

The air was clear and fresh and the sun shining today as Lela and Diana walked away from the Johnson's home. "Let's go to the Café Skyros. I want you to meet someone very special."

"It's that man, isn't it?" Diana asked, her voice held a note of aversion.

"His name is André Stephanos and he happens to be a very *successful* man." Lela walked quickly as she spoke, forcing Diana to keep up with her. She was anxious for her niece to meet André.

"My mother told me that he is looking for a Greek wife. Why hasn't he married one of the many other Greek girls that are already here?" Diana asked what she felt was a practical question.

"He hasn't found the right one yet, that's all."

"So then he may not think I'm the right one either, right?"

"We'll see. From what he's told me, I think you're exactly what he wants in a wife. You're young and unspoiled and you're very beautiful. You're also a good-natured person, which will be helpful to him with his business."

"Aunt Lela, I don't want to marry just anyone. I want to marry Nikoli!"

"Who in the world is Nikoli?" Lela asked impatiently. She didn't have time for her niece's romantic notions.

"He is the most wonderful, loving, and handsome boy in the entire world and I'm saving myself for him."

They had been walking as they conversed, but then Lela stopped abruptly. Although there were other pedestrians passing by, she paid no attention. Placing both hands on Diana's shoulders, Lela looked straight into Diana's eyes. "Now, you listen to me you silly, foolish little girl. Life is not like one of those fatuous books that you read. It is unpredictable and frightening. When an opportunity such as this comes along, you *don't* take it lightly."

Diana was unable to move, blinking back frightened tears. Her aunt had never spoken to her this way before. Up until now, she had been friendly and caring.

Lela let go of Diana's shoulders, turned on the heel of one foot, and continued walking. Diana followed although instead of walking by her aunt's side, she lagged behind.

Diana's mind swirled with a tangle of unanswered questions and confusing thoughts. A young woman in the 1940's had few choices. Add to that being unfamiliar with the country, its customs, and its language, and it was paralyzing.

Homesickness washed over Diana like a gigantic tidal wave, sucking her into the undertow and drowning her emotionally. She couldn't run and hide because there was no where she knew of to run to. She couldn't make the war disappear—the war that had taken Nikoli from her leaving her to fight this emotional battle alone. She felt desperately helpless to change her situation.

"Here we are. Remember to be on your best behavior." Lela reminded Diana reproachfully, then opened the door to the café.

In many ways, the Café Skyros was similar to the Café Parthenon. There was a long black-and-white-tiled counter with twelve red and chrome barstools that swiveled. The front of the Café Skyros faced a busy street and there were four large windows with tables and chairs set up along them so that patrons could look out while they ate. More tables lined the far wall and a row of tables ran up the center.

In Greece with its fairly steady climate, The Café Parthenon had tables with umbrellas and chairs set up outside, but that would have seemed impractical here given the drastic changes in weather in Chicago and the busy street the café was located on.

"Lela!" André greeted her with a warm and hearty welcome. Diana thought he was much more handsome in person than in his picture.

"This must be your niece. Welcome to America and to the Café Skyros. Why don't you ladies have a seat and I'll get you something to drink?" Lela and Diana took off their coats, hung them on the coat rack, and sat down.

By the time Lela had returned to her seat at the counter, André already had a hot cup of coffee waiting for her. Turning to Diana he asked, "Would you like coffee? Or perhaps I could bring you a soda."

"I'd like a cherry phosphate, please." Diana had heard the girls talking about cherry phosphates on her trip across the ocean. She hoped that she liked the way it tasted, but even if she didn't she would drink it so that André wouldn't think she was rude.

André smiled at Diana's ability to make a quick decision. "One cherry phosphate, coming right up." He went to fill her order.

"He likes you already, I can tell," Lela said under her breath.

Diana didn't respond. She was determined to remain loyal to Nikoli.

André returned with the cherry phosphate served in a tall glass with a long spoon and a straw. He placed a beverage napkin down and set the glass on top of it. Noticing that Diana was studying a menu, he asked. "How about something to eat—my treat?"

"I'll have my usual." Lela said.

"Greek omelet?" André confirmed. Lela nodded and smiled.

"I would like a cheeseburger, please." Diana said, setting the menu down. Lela and André both looked at her in surprise.

"Diana, are you sure?" Her niece was full of surprises, Lela thought. She knew that Diana would not have had the opportunity to have a cheeseburger in Greece.

"Yes, I've never had one and I'd like to try it."

"She seems very sure of herself, Lela. That's a good thing for a young woman." André said, writing the order down and heading off towards the kitchen window to put the ticket on the order wheel.

"Is that how he lets the cook know what we want?" Diana was amazed that André had not shouted out to the cook or gone in the back to help prepare the food himself as her father would have done.

"Yes. Things are different here."

While they waited for their food, the café filled up with people. In fact, it got so busy that there were people waiting in line to be seated.

André placed the two plates of hot, fresh food in front of Lela and Diana.

"I hope you both enjoy your meals. Diana, it was a pleasure to meet you. Please come back and visit me again. Now, if you'll excuse me, I have to attend to business."

He nodded in the direction of the doorway where yet more people were coming in.

ॐ

"Well, how did you like your cheeseburger?" Lela asked Diana as they walked home from the café. They had eaten rather quickly to make room for the other customers. After all, André had so generously paid for their meals, it didn't seem right to linger.

"I think it is my new favorite food," Diana said enthusiastically.

"And, what did you think of André? Isn't he handsome?"

"He's okay. He's better looking in person than in that picture my mother showed me." Diana agreed reluctantly.

"I can tell he likes you, we'll have to go back again to visit him. That way you two can get to know each other better."

After her aunt's earlier outburst, Diana didn't dare disagree. "The food is good there and I like the atmosphere. He does a good business - like my father's cafe."

"Yes, he is very successful."

They walked the rest of the way home in silence. Diana thinking of Nikoli, and Lela thinking of the beautiful home she could live in if everything went according to her plan.

CHAPTER SEVEN

ATHENS, OCTOBER 1940

When Nikoli had first arrived at the army training camp on mainland Greece, he had been educated in the use of firearms and explosives. After only one week of rigorous training, he was sent to a camp near the action to wait for his turn to fight on the front line. He had never been more nervous or excited in his life.

Each morning when Nikoli awoke, his first thought was of Diana, and at night, she was the last thing he thought of before drifting off to sleep. His dreams were often filled with her image.

When it was Nikoli's turn to head to the front line with his troop, he fought bravely and valiantly. The rocky mountain terrain made the battle even more difficult. Surrounded by death, he kept his focus on the promise he had made to Diana to return to her unharmed.

Within a few short months, the Greek army successfully drove the Italians back over the border. Their strength and persistence had paid off.

෧

The ship sailing back to Crete was full of exultant men, high from their victory and anxious to return to the women and families they had left behind. Two full months had passed, and Nikoli was eager to see Diana. He had written many poems for her during the lonely nights at war, and he planned to re-write his favorite one on parchment and present it to Diana at Christmas which was only days away.

"There it is!" One of the men cried out upon seeing the island of Crete. The others joined in a loud victory cheer.

The ship was greeted by family and friends. Music filled the air and flowers were strewn upon the men as they disembarked. Nikoli looked around wildly for Diana. Smiling expectantly at first, and then, heart sinking when he realized she was not among the crowd.

"Nikoli!" It was his mother. She was a small, overweight and overbearing woman.

"Mama," he hugged her tightly. Then, noticing that someone accompanied his mother, he nodded in acknowledgement to the young woman.

"This is Sophia. She has been staying with me while you were away." Nikoli was an only child and his mother had always longed for a daughter who could help her maintain the household, just as Nikoli now helped his father with their fishing business.

"It's a pleasure to meet you," Nikoli said politely.

Sophia blushed and looked down at the ground. "It's nice to meet you, too." Unlike Diana in almost every way, Sophia was shy and soft-spoken. Although she was pretty, she lacked the spirit and vivid beauty of Diana.

"We should get home. Your father insisted on preparing a special feast for your return." Catherine Agorinos turned and led the way back to their home with Sophia obediently by her side.

Nikoli followed behind the two women, never giving up his search of the crowd for Diana.

Nikoli had rehearsed over and over what he would say to Diana's parents when he confronted them. There was no way that Nikoli's mother and father would allow him to go about his own business until he ate with them and gave them a report about the battle. He would have to anxiously endure their conversation before he could go to Diana's house.

As soon as it was politely allowable, Nikoli excused himself from the table. He had never actually gone to Diana's house and knocked on her door, but this was different. He had just returned home from war and he had to see her. A stern-looking man opened the door of Diana's home.

"Good evening sir, my name is Nikoli and I'm here to see Diana." He could feel his confidence waver slightly under Constantine's scrutiny.

"She isn't here."

"When will she return?" In answer, Constantine closed the door in his face. Nikoli swallowed hard trying to control his mounting tension.

Standing on the front step wondering what he should do next, he decided it would be best not to cause trouble, although he felt a great urge to pound on the front door with his fists until the door was opened again and he got some answers.

So far, his first night home had been anti-climatic. In his dreams while away at war, Diana had greeted him at the docks. Her beautiful, smiling eyes seeking his. They would embrace and shed tears of sheer joy.

Instead, Nikoli had ended up going to sleep early in hopes that he would find her down by the beach in the morning. Just as he had in the past.

The following morning, Nikoli awoke with the sun, anxious to go to the sea.

Like a madman, he walked up and down the long, sandy beach. Diana was nowhere to be seen. Cursing under his breath at his misfortune, he decided to return to Diana's house.

This time when Constantine answered the door, Nikoli would proclaim his love for Diana and convince her parents that he could love and care for her in the same way she had become accustomed to. Surely, they would listen to what he had to say.

Boldly, he walked up to Diana's house and knocked on the heavy wooden door.

This time, it was Isadora who opened it. "Yes?"

"Please, may I speak with you for a moment?"

"Do I know you?"

"My name is Nikoli Agorinos. My father and I own our own fishing boat. I met Diana down by the beach nearly six months ago. She has come to mean a great deal to me." So far, everything he said was coming out as he had planned.

"Diana is not here. She has gone to America." Isadora would not allow herself to be moved by this young man's foolish talk.

Nikoli retreated slightly at Isadora's words, which made him feel as though she had struck him in the face. "But, why?"

"She was offered a beautiful home and plenty of money to go there and marry a man who owns a café in Chicago."

"Married? Diana's married?" Nikoli spoke in a strangled voice.

"Yes. In fact, she is expecting her first child." It was a lie, but Isadora felt she must do everything she could to protect her daughter from this boy who had no idea how great a responsibility a wife and children really were.

Having heard more than he could possibly bear, Nikoli backed away from the door, while still facing Isodora. "Please, when you write to her, would you tell her that her friend, Nikoli, has returned safely from the war?"

"Yes, of course." Isadora replied quickly, then shut the door firmly, leaving Nikoli standing on the doorstep, bewildered.

In a daze, Nikoli headed for home. All of his hopes and dreams had been spilled into the thirsty dust of life, which seemed to greedily soak them up. For months, his every thought and reason for doing anything had been about Diana. How could she have done this to him? To *them*? It was a cruel betrayal of their love.

Nikoli's heart refused to accept the overwhelming truth of what he had just been told, yet his mind told him otherwise. Eyes darkened with pain, senses dulled, he returned home.

Catherine Agorinos had heard through the gossip mill at the market that her son was smitten with the young, high-spirited, Diana. She knew that such a girl would not make a suitable wife for her Nikoli. Her son needed a woman who could cook, clean and bear him a child—preferably a son, who could also learn the fishing business and carry on the Agorinos tradition.

No, Diana was not the girl for Nikoli. On the other hand, Sophia was exactly what Nikoli needed. Of course, Catherine knew she needed time to convince Nikoli of this fact. When she had seen Sophia at the market, Catherine decided to ask the young girl to help her with the household chores. Sophia was the daughter of a poor farmer, and the offer of extra money, which would go directly to Sophia's father, gave them no choice but to agree to Catherine's request.

Sophia had met and exceeded Catherine's expectations. Her ability to cook, clean, wash clothes, and sew were excellent. She had even managed to teach Catherine a few things. Indeed, this was the perfect girl for her son to marry.

When Nikoli reached his house, he staggered up the two steps that led to the front door. His breathing was ragged and he could barely muster up the strength to pull the door open.

"Nikoli!" Catherine cried out when she saw him.

Nikoli's face, which was usually tanned and healthy looking, was pale and drawn. His eyes were glazed and distant.

"Leave me alone." With unseeing eyes, Nikoli waved his hand limply at his mother who had started towards him. Nikoli swayed, then staggered to his bedroom.

"Go fetch the doctor," Catherine ordered Sophia who immediately ran out the door towards the village.

Catherine placed a pan of water on the stove to boil in order to make an elixir out of herbs. She wasn't exactly sure what was wrong with her son, but a cup of Hyssop tea might soothe him. The doctor would provide further help. Catherine took the tea in to Nikoli but he refused to drink it. He lay on his bed, curled up as though in pain. Sitting on the edge of his bed, Catherine tried urging her son to tell her what was wrong.

"Please tell me what's happened."

"I don't want to talk about it," Nikoli spat out contemptuously, as he lay facing the wall.

Deciding it was futile to continue badgering Nikoli, Catherine left him.

When the doctor arrived with Sophia, he peered into Nikoli's eyes, looked into his mouth, and listened to his heart. "There is nothing wrong with this man. He is as healthy as can be! I suggest you give him an herbal preparation that will relax him. He is in shock after returning home from the war. He'll be fine once he adjusts again."

Nikoli was in shock, but not for the reason that the doctor had suggested.

There was no herbal medicine that could cure him.

The strange thing was that he was unable to cry and yet, the pain and anguish of war were unequalled to that which he suffered now.

CHAPTER EIGHT

Christmas had come and gone. Despite the terrible news of Diana, Nikoli had chosen his favorite poem from the many that he had written to her while away at war and carefully rewrote it on parchment. After allowing the ink to dry, he rolled the paper and secured it with a piece of red ribbon he had found in his mother's sewing box.

In his bedroom, Nikoli removed a piece of stone from the wall. He had hollowed out the area behind it as a secret hiding place. Removing a small wooden box that held other mementos, he placed the rolled parchment inside, but not before looking at some of the other items inside the box.

There was a rock from the beach. It was the most beautiful shade of dark green blending into teal and blue. Diana had found it and given it to him in memory of their time spent together near the sea. Nikoli remembered telling Diana that the green reminded him of the color of her eyes.

The second item was a bird's feather, which Diana had playfully run across his cheek.

The last item caused him to draw in a sharp intake of breath. It was a purple flower that Diana had worn in her hair and had given to Nikoli. He could see her removing it from her thick, dark hair, eyes never leaving his, and handing the flower to him.

The flower was dried up now and the scent was gone. *Just like Diana's love for me*, Nikoli thought.

Sensing the approaching feeling of desperation and hopelessness, he quickly closed the box and returned it to its hiding place.

Throughout the following months Nikoli became more withdrawn from his surroundings. He returned to work with his father on the fishing boat finding the familiarity of the daily routine comforting.

Jason Agorinos was a quiet, hard-working man. The name Jason, which means 'gentle, healing spirit', befitted him. He had learned to fish as a young boy off of the boat of a wealthy man who had owned a fleet of fishing boats. When Jason was eighteen, he bought his first boat and had successfully built his business in his hometown.

Jason had a reputation for catching and selling some of the finest seafood. The men who worked for him respected him and gave him a fair-days' work. Nikoli enjoyed working with his father. Because he was the boss's son, he always toiled harder and longer than the other men. Nikoli felt that he had to prove his worth because one day he knew he would take over his father's business.

Sophia had become a surprising comfort to Nikoli. She mended his clothes and made new shirts for him. In the kitchen, Sophia helped Catherine prepare Nikoli's favorite meals. To his delight, she too had a love for poetry, which she often shared with the family in the evening after supper.

One night, after a particularly touching poem that Sophia had recited in front of the family, Nikoli sat lost in thought, staring at her. Sensing the possibilities, Catherine and her husband left the room, leaving the two young people alone.

"That was beautiful, Sophia," Nikoli said, his voice soft and sincere.

"Thank you. I wrote it after my mother died." She looked down shyly, her cheeks burning from his compliment.

"Life on a farm is hard work." Nikoli said knowingly.

"Yes. There is so much to do. Looking after the flocks, joining in the harvest, and grinding the grain into flour was all very tiring. I'm grateful that your mother asked me to come and help her. The money she pays my father each month helps him and the rest of my family greatly."

It was more than Sophia had ever spoken to Nikoli. Aware of his eyes on her, she blushed again.

"You are a joy to have around. My mother loves you like a daughter, I can see that." Nikoli's eyes held both admiration as well as a hint of seduction.

Sophia smiled and looked up at him, sensing his mood. "I should go to bed, it's late."

"No. Please wait." Nikoli had surprised himself as well as Sophia by his urgent request. Something within him longed for her to stay and talk to him some more. Maybe it was his loneliness, or his need for female attention. Whatever it was, he wasn't ready to part company with her just yet.

"What is it?" She had begun to rise up off of the sofa where she'd been sitting, but had sat back down at his request.

Nikoli walked over to sit next to her. Without warning, he kissed her on the lips, softly at first and then more intently.

Sophia had never kissed a man before. Of course, she had given her father good night kisses on the cheek, and her uncles were greeted with a kiss hello or good-bye.

Never, not even in her imagination, had she dreamed of kissing or being kissed like this.

She was intrigued and repulsed all at once.

Pushing him firmly away, she said in a choked voice, "Nikoli, please stop."

"Forgive me, Sophia." He ran a hand through his hair, got up and started to pace the room.

Nikoli had upset her balance and her mind was reeling. Sophia left the room swiftly and Nikoli heard her bedroom door shut firmly behind her.

That night, Sophia lay in her bed, reliving Nikoli's kiss, and felt the blood coursing through her veins. He had awakened in her a passion that she had never dared to acknowledge. It was at that moment, she realized, that she had fallen hopelessly in love with Nikoli.

In his own bed, Nikoli lay cursing himself in the darkness. He felt like a traitor.

How could he kiss another woman when he still loved Diana? How could he still love Diana when she was married to another man, and expecting his child, thousands of miles away?

Eventually, he knew, he would have to seek the comfort of another woman's arms. Sophia was pretty, smart, and hard-working. He could see that she would make any man a good wife.

Besides, there was talk that the victory of the Greek army was short-lived. The Germans were joining forces with Italy in their attempt to invade Greece. It was very possible that he would have to return to war.

That night, Nikoli fell asleep and dreamed not of Diana, but of Sophia.

CHAPTER NINE

GREECE, FEBRUARY 1941

In late February of 1941, Sophia and Nikoli became man and wife. They had a large wedding with many of the people that fished with Nikoli and his father in attendance.

Wine flowed and platters, overflowing with food, were served. Men and women alike wished the newlywed couple well.

Nikoli looked over at Sophia who was talking to one of his relatives. She was overwhelmingly beautiful today in her white, handmade wedding dress. On her head was a wreath of flowers that accentuated her dark hair, which was elegantly pulled up into a twist emphasizing her high cheekbones and almond-shaped eyes.

Nikoli swore to himself, as he had a million times before, that he would do well by her. Sophia deserved the best he had to offer. It wasn't her fault that Diana had stolen his heart and he'd never been able to retrieve it. Nikoli valiantly fought off any thoughts of Diana. Today of all days he would not allow himself to think of her, it would be a betrayal to Sophia.

Sophia caught his eye and smiled at him, then blushed. She had never loved anyone in the world as much as she loved Nikoli. He looked so handsome in his black suit and white shirt. His full head of wavy, dark hair was combed neatly back, and his dusky eyes held their usual glint of mischief.

It had taken many weeks for Nikoli to realize and accept that Diana was gone and not coming back. Sophia had often seen Diana in the village, but had never spoken with her. Diana's beauty was the talk of the town and many of the young boys had crushes on her. She had a lively independent spirit that men admired and women envied.

Sophia hadn't known of Diana's association with Nikoli until the day she had picked up the mail for Catherine at the post office. There was only one piece of mail - a letter - and it was addressed to Nikoli.

Upon returning home, Sophia had handed the letter to Catherine who had immediately grown pale and faint. Practically falling back into one of the kitchen chairs, she held the letter away from her as though it were a disgusting, vile thing. In a choked voice, Catherine had ordered Sophia to burn the letter. "Quickly, throw this into the fire!"

Walking over to the fireplace, Sophia pretended to throw the letter into the flames, but instead placed the letter into the deep pocket on the front of her skirt. Thankfully, Catherine was in too much distress to notice. Fetching a glass of water, Sophia handed it to Catherine who was still sitting in the chair in a daze.

Once she was in the privacy of her own bedroom, Sophia had read the letter and tucked it away inside a book of poems which she kept in her box of keepsakes. She wasn't sure why she even kept the letter, but she knew she must never let Nikoli see it. Whenever a letter came addressed to Nikoli from America, Sophia would read it then hide it with the others, never telling Catherine of her duplicity.

Catherine had made no secret of the fact that she had hoped for Nikoli and Sophia to become husband and wife. Nikoli would never go against his parent's wishes and run off to America to chase after a girl that his parents didn't approve of. Sophia had accepted early on that if Nikoli did marry her, she would become his wife by default—not because he was deeply in love with her as he had been with Diana. Being a simple girl, Sophia didn't care. She had already experienced a much better life after coming to live with Catherine and anything else that came with it would have been considered her great fortune.

Because of the war, Nikoli and Sophia had decided against going away on a honeymoon. Instead, a friend of Nikoli's father had offered the use of his home by the sea to the newlyweds as his wedding gift to them. He had business to tend to and would be miles away in another town for the following week. Gratefully, Nikoli and Sophia had accepted.

Jason Agorinos had generously loaned Nikoli the use of his horse and cart for the next five days. He would rely on one of the men he worked with to transport his daily catch into town. It was well after midnight when they reached the home where they would spend their honeymoon. Nikoli felt a wave of apprehension as he helped Sophia down from the cart. He reached in to gather their canvas bags and carried them up to the house as Sophia followed behind him.

"All that socializing has worn me out, how about you, are your tired?" Nikoli asked, hoping that for once Sophia would show some sign of *not* wanting to be with him.

"No, actually, I think I'm too excited to sleep!" She couldn't wait to be alone with him. She had heard many stories of a man and wife's first night together. The women who had married kind men always had wonderful things to say about their wedding night and she felt that Nikoli fell into this category. He had always been gentle and understanding with her and she felt confident that tonight would be no exception.

The house was laid out identically to Nikoli's parents' house with the only difference being a balcony off of the kitchen overlooking the sea. Someone had thoughtfully left an oil lamp burning in the kitchen for the young couple.

Nikoli stood awkwardly in the center of the main living area of the home. "I guess I should put these in the bedroom." He said, holding up their bags.

"I'll take mine so that I can get what I need out of it. I'll use the washroom to change. Would you please unfasten the buttons on the back of my dress for me?" Sophia waited patiently while Nikoli clumsily unbuttoned the small, smooth buttons of her wedding dress. Once the task was completed, she took her bag and went in the direction of where she thought the bathroom was situated. Finding it, she turned and smiled shyly at Nikoli before closing the door.

Nikoli loosened his necktie and unbuttoned his shirt. He knew that he was supposed to want to make love to his new wife, but where was his desire? He did love Sophia, but it was a different kind of love that he felt for her compared to the love he had felt for Diana.

All night he had struggled to chase away thoughts of Diana. He had to train his mind to focus on his future—and his future was with Sophia. He could hear her in the washroom, moving about, and he could sense her excitement and anticipation.

Removing the rest of his clothes and laying them neatly over a chair in the corner of the room, Nikoli went over to the bed. When Sophia opened the door to the washroom, she looked around the room for Nikoli and blushed when she saw him already lying down.

She wore a flowing white, knee-length, sleeveless cotton nightgown. The neckline fell to a deep "V", revealing her full round breasts. Her long, dark hair was brushed smooth and hung loosely about her shoulders. She looked and felt very beautiful as she made her way over to the bed to join her husband.

Nikoli smiled apprehensively at her. It didn't seem right that he should feel more nervous than she. He pulled the covers down so that Sophia could slip in beside him.

"Darling, you look very beautiful." He meant it, however this affirmation was not registering as it should have on the rest of his body.

Smiling pensively, Sophia lay on the bed next to Nikoli who was leaning on his elbow looking at her, she smiled up at him. "Thank you. I wanted tonight to be special."

"It has already been a special night for me. Thank you for marrying me, I hope I will be a good husband to you."

"Nikoli, of course you will be, just as I will be a good wife to you. We will have a wonderful life together." She longed for him to end his talking and kiss her.

"I'm very tired and would like to go to sleep, I think I may have drank too much wine." Instead of a night full of romance and passion, Nikoli kissed her chastely on the lips and fell asleep.

Sophia lay in the darkness wondering what she had done wrong. Silent tears of anger and embarrassment coursed down her cheeks as she looked over at Nikoli's sleeping form.

Though the window was shut to keep out the chilly night air, she could hear the soothing sound of gentle waves lapping against the beach. Forcing her mind to listen to the steady rhythm of the water instead of the confusing and agonizing thoughts in her head, Sophia finally drifted off to sleep.

The next morning brought with it the sunshine. The air was still cool, but spring comes early to Crete, and it wouldn't be long before the weather warmed up again. Nikoli insisted that they walk into town and eat breakfast.

"I was hoping we could take a romantic walk along the beach," Sophia said.

"There's nothing there that I haven't seen a million times before. That is where I work!" *And that is where I spent many hours with Diana in the late afternoon.*

With a small pout, Sophia agreed and took Nikoli's outstretched hand. They walked into town and had breakfast at the local *taverna*, the only other place to eat besides Diana's fathers' café.

After breakfast, the two of them walked through the *liekey*, the open-air market, and bought fresh fruits and vegetables to snack on later in the day.

Nikoli was recognized by one of the men at the fruit stand. "Congratulations! I had heard you were getting married. This must be your lovely bride, Diana!"

Dimitri waited for an introduction. He and Nikoli had fought in the war together and the two men had each talked about the women in their lives. It was only natural that he would think the woman with Nikoli was Diana.

"Dimitri, I would like you to meet Sophia," Nikoli said, unable to miss the crushed look in Sophia's eyes.

Confusion flashed in Dimitri's eyes, but he quickly recovered. "Sophia, it is my deepest pleasure to meet you. Please, I would like to give you a gift." Grabbing a bouquet of flowers from the stand next to his, he handed them to Sophia with a flourish.

Sophia took the flowers from him and buried her nose in the bouquet, an act of accepting his apology for his earlier blunder. "They smell wonderful, thank you!"

The demand of other customers took Dimitri away to take care of business, but just as Nikoli and Sophia were getting ready to walk away, he called out to them, "I hear that we may have to go back and fight. The German's have joined forces with Italy."

"I heard. We will not think of war today, though." Nikoli did not want to think of guns and death the day after his wedding.

"Of course you don't. Forgive me again. I'll be seeing you then." Dimitri turned back to his responsibilities at the fruit stand.

The remainder of their first day together was spent walking through the village. When they had seen enough, they returned to the home they were borrowing for a nap before supper.

While Nikoli lay on the bed, Sophia arranged the fresh flowers in a clay vase she found in one of the cupboards. The fresh fruit was put into a large wooden bowl and left on the kitchen table. Peeling an orange and placing it on a plate, Sophia made her way over to the bed where Nikoli had laid down.

He was asleep already, and she was able to study him openly. Sophia drank him in with her eyes. She reached a hand out to touch his thick, dark hair. With his eyes closed, his long, dark lashes fanned against his cheek.

His lips curved deliciously in a perpetual smile, even while at rest. Sophia ran a finger along the square edge of his jaw wanting to kiss him, feeling afraid at first, then boldly yet gently she pressed her lips against his. Nikoli's eyes lazily opened halfway.

Startled, as though she had been caught doing something wrong, Sophia started to move away, but Nikoli reached out and caught her by the wrist, pulling her gently back down on the bed.

Rolling over onto his right side, he pressed his body to hers, kissing her slowly at first, his tongue sending shivers of desire racing through her until Sophia thought she could stand no more. She could feel the blood pulsing through her body. Every part of her was alive and awake to Nikoli.

Sophia had never been with a man before, but she was ready for Nikoli. She made no attempt to hide the fact that she wanted him as the caress of his lips on her mouth and along her body set her aflame. Her moan of desire seemed to drive him on.

Although his eyes were closed, he was kissing her everywhere, touching her everywhere, driving her mad with passion. Her heart was pounding as though it would explode. "Nikoli!" she cried out, desperately needing more of him.

"Shhh" he quieted her with his mouth. He didn't want to talk or think. He only wanted to feel, and pretend that it was Diana he was loving.

CHAPTER TEN

When it was time to leave the house by the sea, Sophia wistfully looked around and sighed. If only she and Nikoli could stay here alone instead of returning to his parents' home. Of course, she was grateful for a place to live, but she really wanted to have a home of her own and start a family. Sophia had promised Catherine that she would stay on a while longer because she knew that the older woman had become dependent upon her help. Fortunately, she and Catherine got along well and Sophia's new mother-in-law had more than approved of the marriage.

Upon Nikoli and Sophia's return, they were greeted with hugs and kisses as well as a huge meal. There was roasted lamb, beans with almonds cooked in olive oil, and a fresh salad with tomatoes, cucumbers, carrots, topped with crumbled feta cheese. The air was filled with the aroma of basil, thyme, and oregano.

"Look at what a beautiful couple you make! I'm so proud of you both. Are you hungry? I've been cooking all day." Catherine didn't wait for an answer. Filling two plates with food, she set them in front of Nikoli and Sophia then returned to the stove to prepare a plate for herself and her husband.

The four of them sat together talking of the wedding, the people who had attended, and the gifts the newlywed couple had received.

After dinner, Nikoli and his father left the ladies to clean up and went for a walk and a cigarette. Although Jason Agorinos was a quiet man, he was also very perceptive.

His son had worked by his side since he was a child and he knew this boy-turned-man very well.

Jason took the pack of cigarettes from the breast pocket of his shirt, offering it first to Nikoli then taking one out for himself. Without saying a word, he lit both with a match and inhaled deeply, savoring the smell of burning tobacco.

Both men walked and smoked their cigarettes in silence for a while. When they had reached the craggy rocks that overlooked the sea, Jason finally spoke. "Our victory against Italy was short-lived. The Germans have joined forces with the Italians. The Germans are very powerful and I am afraid we will not be successful this time."

"Yes, we will. I'll fight to defend my country."

"I don't want you to volunteer. You just got married and I need you here to help me with the business. We could feign that you are ill."

"It's my duty to go. Our army will need all the manpower it can get."

Jason looked out over the sea. The sun was sinking lower, streaks of orange and violet painted the early evening sky. "What can I do or say that would make you change your mind?"

"Father, what choice do I have? If I don't go, I'll be branded a coward!"

It was true. Every young and able-bodied man was expected to join forces against the enemy to protect their country. Nikoli would not be able to show his face in public without shame if he didn't go to war.

"I have a bad feeling," Jason put his fist to his gut in a gesture of grief. "This war is going to go on much longer than we anticipated, and it is going to get uglier."

"Nonsense. We beat them before and we'll do it again." Nikoli drew in on his cigarette, confident of what he was saying.

"I wish I could be so sure." Jason took one more drag from his cigarette before throwing it to the ground and crushing it with the heel of his shoe. Looking over at his son who was quietly looking out to sea, he said, "Let's go see if your mother has any dessert for us." Jason led the way back towards the house.

❧

February gave way to March as Nikoli and Sophia grew to know one another as husband and wife. Each day for Sophia was spent going to the market, cooking, cleaning and sewing with Catherine. Sophia loved taking care of Nikoli and she made sure that every single one of his needs was met.

In late March, every man in Greece capable of fighting was called away to war.

Germany had become more aggressive in helping Italy gain access to the Greek seaports.

The Agorinos' home was filled with great sadness the morning that Nikoli set out to leave. Catherine had fixed him a delicious breakfast of fresh bread, eggs with onion and cheese, and strong black coffee.

One by one, they said their good-byes to Nikoli. Each with their own private wish for his safe return.

"My son, I pray you will return safely to us. May Hermes, the protector of travelers be with you." Catherine held her son close as she spoke these words over him.

"Son, I know you will fight well. For your family as well as your country." Jason's voice cracked in a rare outward display of emotion.

Catherine and Jason each went outside to tend to an imaginary task in the garden so that Nikoli and Sophia could have a moment alone.

"Nikoli, please don't go! There must be a way out of this." Sophia could barely control her anguish. She loved him more than life itself and the realization that he might not return was agonizing.

"Please, Sophia, don't get so emotional. I'll return. Remember how you and mother greeted me at the seaport last time I came home from the war?" He was holding her close to him, talking into her hair, rubbing her back soothingly.

Looking up at him, tears streaking her cheeks, she said, "Yes, I remember that day. I'll always remember how handsome you were walking down the gangplank towards us."

"And I will do so again. However next time I'll want more than a pleasant handshake from you upon my return." He said huskily, wanting to lighten her mood.

Blushing deeply, she said, "Nikoli,…"

The door opened and without going into the house, Jason called out, "The wagon is here to pick you up and take you to the docks." Once again, Nikoli would be taking a ship to the mainland where the fighting was taking place. And once again, he was saying farewell to a woman that he loved. For he had come to love Sophia, perhaps not with the same passion that he had felt for Diana, but he did love her.

Nikoli turned back to Sophia. "Be brave, and I'll see you very soon, my dear." He kissed her quickly, grabbed his canvas bag of personal belongings, and headed out the door with Sophia following behind him.

Catherine, Jason, and Sophia stood together with their arms around each other for strength, waving good-bye to the wagon full of men.

CHAPTER ELEVEN

As fate would have it, Nikoli was placed once again in the same troop as his friend, Dimitri. The two young men had not seen each other since that day at the market.

For an entire week, those who would fight had been placed through a rigorous training program of running, climbing, and jumping hurdles. Shooting guns, reloading quickly and shooting again.

On the night before Nikoli and Dimitri were to go to the front line, they went into the large tent that was set up for socializing to have a cigarette after dinner.

The tent was noisy, filled with soldiers standing around talking and drinking coffee in a haze of gray cigarette smoke. There were also several card games in progress with men playing in the hopes of winning cigarettes or a magazine.

"That was some mistake I made at the market. I'm sorry if I embarrassed you and your wife." Dimitri said, then lit his cigarette.

Nikoli gave him an understanding look. "Hey, the last time we fought this war together I spent my entire free time pining away about Diana. How were you to know that I'd end up marrying someone else?"

Dimitri was relieved that his friend was not upset with him. "What happened, then?"

Nikoli struggled to hide the burning anger that still blazed within him whenever he thought about what Diana had done. "She…she went to America."

"To get away from the war," Dimitri was not surprised. Many Greeks were fleeing to the safety and promise of wealth in America.

"She went there to marry a café owner who offered her a life that I could never give her."

"What?" Dimitri asked in disbelief. "You should have gone after her. I certainly would have if it were my girl."

"Her mother said that she was already expecting their first child."

Dimitri's face fell, his eyes widened. From the stories that Nikoli had told him about Diana, he was sure that the girl was as much in love with Nikoli as he was with her. Love was an unpredictable thing.

"Didn't she leave you a letter or something?"

"No. There was nothing from her. I'd hoped she would have written to me and at least tell me herself why she had made the decision she'd made."

"I still say you should have gone after her. Maybe there was still something you could have done to change her mind."

Nikoli didn't reply, but inhaled deeply from his cigarette with a vague, faraway look in his eyes.

"That leads us to Sophia, then. How did you come to know her?" Dimitri asked.

"When I returned home from the war, my mother introduced me to her. She is the daughter of a poor farmer whose wife had died and left him with three children. Sophia is the middle child and she was willing to come to work for my mother and help her with the household. In return, my mother sends Sophia's father money every week so that he can purchase items that he cannot produce on his farm."

"Well, she's very pretty, and she seems to be good-natured." Dimitri said reflectively, remembering the young woman who had been with Nikoli that day at the market.

"Yes, she is." Nikoli looked away so that the other man could not read the expression in his eyes.

Sensing what he was feeling, Dimitri said, "But she is not Diana, right?"

Nikoli turned his head sharply so that his eyes met Dimitri's. "No, she doesn't have the same spirit and love for life that Diana had. But I'm determined to forget the pain and anguish that Diana has caused me. I intend on being a wonderful husband to Sophia."

Dimitri knew that Nikoli's avowal of being a good husband was more for his friend's own benefit. Maybe if he said it often enough he would make good on his promise.

"Let's get this war over with first, then you can concentrate on your marriage."

"Yes, I pray that the gods will be with us. The German's are well-armed, and very powerful." Nikoli said, thoughtfully.

"Our country has faced many wars. We are simply carrying on the fight for our independence."

"I know. I only wish that I didn't have such an awful sense of foreboding." Nikoli had been unable to ward off the sense of tension and anxiety he had felt upon his arrival in Athens. He hadn't felt it the first time he had come to the mainland to fight.

"You shouldn't talk that way. You'll put a hex on our mission." Dimitri threw his cigarette to the ground and crushed it beneath his boot. "Let's get some sleep. We have to be up early in the morning."

After taking one more hit off of his cigarette, Nikoli threw the remainder to the ground and followed Dimitri to the bunkhouse.

ص

The weather in northern Greece is much cooler than Nikoli was accustomed to in Crete. Spring comes much earlier to the southernmost island; it had yet to make its appearance in Athens.

The morning dawned, gray and inhospitable, and a light mist left the air cold and damp. The troop was staked out behind piles of rocks and sandbags. The sergeant, a young man in his late twenties, scanned the terrain with his binoculars. It had been quiet for far too long now. Something was about to happen, he could sense it.

Once more the sergeant panned left, then right, the binoculars magnifying that which was in the distance. As he panned to the right again, his hand froze, body tensed, at the sight before him. With the binoculars still up to his eyes, he let out a gasp. "*Maron!*"

Two German tanks and a wall of men were headed directly towards them. The sergeant looked around at his troops who were mere boys! Most of them had barely reached the age of twenty. Some of them had fallen asleep, others were smoking and talking, waiting for action.

"Attention!" he barked out.

Hearts raced and pounded when the men heard the alert. This was it! This was the moment they had been waiting for—to rid their beloved land of the enemy.

Each group had an appointed leader to whom the sergeant gave orders. "You," he pointed to a group of men that were situated on his right, "take your men and line them up along the road." Then turning to the leader of another group he said, "Have your men spread out among the rocks and hills." Quickly the men scattered to do as they were told.

Picking up his radio, the sergeant signaled to the leader of the men who were already situated across the road. "Did you see what's on its way?"

"Yes. My men are in position."

"Good. Wait until the enemy is upon us before firing. I want a shower of bullets on them, don't stop firing. Do you understand?" If they were going to lose this battle, then they were going to do as much damage as possible first.

There was no way they would be able to fight against the tanks. The best they could do was to take out as many of the soldiers that were on foot. Minutes later, the fighting began when a Greek soldier tossed a grenade at the oncoming adversary, the explosion hurled pieces of the very earth they were defending into the air as the enemy ascended upon them in a swarm.

Machine guns blasted, grenades exploded, and there were shouts and screams of the wounded and dying. Dimitri and Nikoli fought side by side, fighting with courage and determination. Each one covering for the other when they reloaded their guns.

Then it happened—it happened so fast that it didn't seem real at all. One minute Dimitri was fighting the enemy beside Nikoli, the next minute he was forced backward, thrown to the ground as if by an invisible hand.

At first, Nikoli's mind couldn't fully comprehend what had just happened. He knelt down beside Dimitri in the foxhole from which they'd been shooting. Adrenaline pumped through Nikoli's body like a drug, stomach clenched tight, as he peered down at the face of death.

The sight before him tore at his insides, his thinking was shattered. "Nooo!" It was a primitive, wild, unearthly cry that went unheard amidst the surrounding noises of war.

Picking up his machine gun, Nikoli climbed out of the foxhole. Pulling the pin of a grenade as he ran, he threw it into the enemy line. Plunging himself into the heat of the battle, he fired his gun wildly at his opponents, the rat-a-tat-tat of the machine gun sounding like sweet, vengeful music to Nikoli's ears. He could feel the hate running through his blood, burning his soul.

When he felt the bullets rip through his body, throwing him to the ground like a rag doll, the last thing he thought of before his eyes closed was Diana.

It was at that very moment that Diana, who was scrubbing the marble foyer of the Johnson's home, thousands of miles away from the fighting, stopped abruptly to clutch at her stomach. Still on her knees, a bucket of soapy water in front of her, she rocked back and forth in pain.

"Nikoli," she cried out softly, her voice strangled and unnatural. She knew something terrible had happened.

There was no way for her to confirm her premonition.

CHAPTER TWELVE

Diana had sent one letter every month to Nikoli. She also wrote to her parents every month to tell them about her new life in America. Only once did she dare mention Nikoli in one of her letters. Her mother had written back that she had not heard mention of his returning home from the war.

Why hasn't he written to me? Diana wondered, as the months passed by. If only there was a way for her to find out exactly what was going on back home!

She and Nikoli had kept their love for each other a secret, even from their friends. It wasn't acceptable for a girl to meet with a boy in private as she had been, so she hadn't risked telling anyone about their secret trysts.

The only mention of Nikoli she had made was to her father, when he had mentioned sending her to America. And that had been a disaster! Constantine would not stand for his daughter going around with a boy behind his back.

Diana worked with her aunt every day. She liked being busy—it kept her mind off of other things. Every day she would pick up the mail from the mail bin in the downstairs front hallway—and every day she was disappointed because there wasn't a letter from Nikoli.

At the end of each week, on either a Friday or a Saturday morning, Mrs. Johnson paid Diana and Lela. It had become a ritual for them to go straight to the Café Skyros to treat themselves to a meal with their pay.

More often, André was picking up the tab for their meals. It was also becoming apparent to Diana that the man truly admired her, and it would only be a matter of time now that he would want to spend time with her away from the café.

Every month that passed without word from or about Nikoli was like a wedge between them, buffering her heart from the terrible blow she felt must surely be forthcoming.

If he had been killed at war, why wouldn't his mother answer one of the letters she had sent to his home?

Occasionally, Diana had seen the newspapers at the Johnson's home. Every now and then, there would be a news article about the war overseas and how it was still not over. She was aware that the particular battle that Nikoli had fought to hold back the Italians had been victorious, but there were still rumblings that the Germans were planning to send forces to back up the Italian troops to gain access to the Greek seaports.

Diana knew that her aunt and her parents would have squelched any mention of her returning home to Greece.

One morning, in early May of 1941, Diana went to fetch the mail as usual and found a letter addressed to her. It was in her mother's beautiful handwriting and she opened it at once, running up the stairs as she did so that she could read it in private.

April 30, 1941

My Dearest Diana,

I miss you so. It has been quiet here without you, but I know that you are safer there than you would be here in Greece. Our men were unable to fight against the powerful German army and the Germans have moved their troops into Athens They have also taken over our beloved island of Crete and the streets are always guarded by German soldiers. I am not sure how much longer I will be able to correspond with you. Food and water are being rationed.

It is a shame and a disgrace that they have taken down our beloved flag and in its place raised their own flag. I heard tell that in Athens, the soldier who was forced to remove the Greek flag wrapped himself in it and threw himself over a cliff.

Diana paused in her reading momentarily to wonder, with trepidation, if it had been Nikoli who had done such a thing. Deciding that he wouldn't, she continued reading the letter.

I also heard, at the market about a week ago, that the young man you asked about, Nikoli, had gotten married back in February. The girl he married is the daughter of a poor farmer. She had gone to work for Catherine, Nikoli's mother. However, Nikoli and all other able-bodied men had been called back to fight and he has not, as of this letter, returned.

Diana had been sitting at the tiny kitchen table. As she read these final words her mother had written to her she felt as though the entire room were spinning and she slid from her chair onto the floor.

Lela spun around from the counter where she was preparing a light meal for the two of them. "Diana!" she dropped the knife to the counter and ran over to her niece.

"Diana, honey, talk to me. What is it?" Looking at her niece's pale, waxen face and limp form, she realized that someone must have died. Picking up the letter that had dropped to the floor beside Diana, she read it quickly, prepared for the worst.

Reaching the part about Nikoli's marriage, she realized that this is what must have affected her niece. At least her sister and her husband were all right. That's all that mattered to Lela.

"Diana, come on now. I want you to come over to the bed and lie down. I'll get you a cool rag and something to drink."

"No, no!" Diana wailed.

More firmly this time, Lela said, "I can't very well lift you, but I can help you over to the bed. Now, put your arm around me and stand up!"

Diana's eyes fluttered, then opened wide. With frightening strength she started to pummel her aunt. "No, no! Get away from me!"

Lela backed away in fear as she watched Diana completely lose control, rolling back and forth on the floor screaming, pulling at her hair and clothes. She was digging her fingernails into her arms, leaving angry red streaks.

Lela went to fetch her private stash of brandy. Then, kneeling beside Diana, she grabbed the girl firmly by the hair. "Listen to me! You have got to settle down. Now!"

"You're hurting me!" Diana wailed, slapping her aunt's hands away from her.

"Drink this," she held the bottle of brandy to Diana's lips and tipped it.

Diana sipped, choked and sputtered. "That's awful!"

"I don't care, it will help you calm down. Now try again, only this time don't spit it out!" Lela once again held the bottle to Diana's lips, and this time, Diana took a healthy swig of the burning liquid.

"I think I'm going to throw up!" she cried out in agony.

"Let me help you to my bed so you can lie down." Lela set the bottle of brandy onto the table. Placing an arm around Diana, she helped her to a standing position and they both stumbled towards Lela's bedroom.

Once Diana was lying down, Lela removed the girl's shoes and covered her with a blanket. Going into the bathroom, she dampened a wash rag in cold water and went to place it on Diana's forehead.

Sitting on the bed next to Diana, Lela held her hand. "You rest now. Everything will be better tomorrow."

Nothing will ever be right again. Diana thought silently to herself. It was the only thing that was running through her mind as she lay there in shock. She felt cold and numb in body, mind and spirit.

Diana's teeth began to chatter uncontrollably as she lay on the bed staring at the ceiling. Concerned about the hollow, vacant look in her niece's eyes, Lela decided to call for a doctor.

When the doctor arrived, he checked Diana's heart, pulse, throat, ears and eyes. "She appears to have suffered a nervous breakdown. Her reflexes are somewhat slow, but that could be temporary. Some people snap back quickly and others never do at all. She's young, though, and that is in her favor."

He opened his black medical bag and took out a bottle of white pills. Shaking out a handful of them, he placed them in a white envelope and printed Diana's name on it as well as instructions. "Give her one of these every four hours. It will help her to relax and get some rest. We'll know in a few days whether or not she'll pull through."

The doctor closed his medical bag with an authoritarian snap, placed his hat on his head and said good day.

Lela shook out one of the pills from the envelope, filled a glass with water, and watched as Diana swallowed the medicine.

Throughout the night, Lela tended to Diana when she cried out. Every four hours, as the doctor had prescribed, she gave Diana one of the white pills, which helped her to relax and fall back to sleep.

The following morning was bright and sunny, contrary to the mood that prevailed in Diana's heart. She looked over at her aunt who was sleeping on a chair in the corner of the bedroom, vaguely remembering that Lela had been there throughout the night when she'd had her nightmares.

"Auntie Lela, wake up, it's late. We'll be late for work." Diana said as she forced herself into a sitting position and as she did so, her head began to spin again and she felt weak.

Lela opened her eyes, not quite focusing on anything in particular at first. Then noticing Diana sitting up, she cried out in relief, "Oh, darling! You're going to be okay!"

Shaking off sleep, Lela went over to the bed and sat next to Diana putting her arms around her. "I was so worried about you. I was so afraid!" Lela was trying not to cry, yet her voice quavered as she spoke.

Diana coldly pushed Lela's hand away. "Please, don't. I don't want another word spoken about what happened."

"If you say so." Lela pulled back in incredulity. Could this be the same person who had entirely lost control of herself only yesterday? "Let's get ourselves washed up and be on our way to work then. I'll apologize to Mrs. Johnson for being late and we can make it up to her on Saturday if she likes."

Silently, Diana got up to wash and dress herself. She moved slowly, as though each action required great thought. Lela recognized the sign of a broken spirit.

"Hey, what do you say we treat ourselves to a mid-week dinner out tonight? We can afford it, now that there's two of us paying the bills." Lela tried to lighten Diana's frame of mind.

In monotone, Diana replied, "Whatever you'd like aunt Lela." She was putting on her shoes and didn't bother to look up when she spoke.

Once they were outside, Diana allowed herself to delight in the warm spring air. It was a welcome reminder of new beginnings, and that was exactly what she was going to have to do. Begin again.

This is what happens to people, Diana thought. *This is the kind of thing that puts a bitter look on a person's face, and an empty look in their eyes. The death of a loved one, and the death of love.*

Diana would never be the same after reading her mother's letter. A part of her soul had been vanquished. She had passed over the line from being a happy, silly naïve girl to becoming a woman, with all of the pain that accompanied adulthood.

Suddenly seeing her aunt through different eyes, Diana realized the grief she must have suffered when her husband had been drowned at sea. She understood now why Lela had felt the desire to come to America and seek her fortune.

Lela caught the pensive look in Diana's eyes and smiled at her. This time, Diana smiled back.

CHAPTER THIRTEEN

"Ladies, what brings you to grace my presence with your beauty mid-week?"

André greeted Lela and Diana as they walked through the door of the Café Skyros.

"We're having a rough week and need a pick-me-up." Lela answered, genially.

André looked at Diana who seemed withdrawn and pale. "Bad news from home?" he asked. He was more accurate in his assumption than he could have known.

"We just learned firsthand that Germany has taken over Athens and Crete. I was hoping the war would be over by now." Lela replied.

"There will always be wars. That's one thing in life that you can be sure of. It's only a matter of time before the United States becomes involved. Now, what can I get for you tonight? The treat's on me."

"No, really André, that's not necessary. You've been so generous already."

"I insist. Especially since I would like to ask you and Diana to go to the movie house with me on Saturday night."

"We'd be delighted! Oh, André, we need a big dose of fun right now. Thank you."

"Thank *you*! I look forward to you and Diana coming in to the café, it's the highlight of my entire week." He looked at Diana specifically when he said this, his golden brown eyes meeting her own and locking for a moment before Diana glanced down shyly.

Lela quietly acknowledged the unspoken message that had passed between them. "Well, I guess I'll have a cheeseburger for a change. Diana, will you be having your usual?"

"Yes, please." Diana said, grateful that her aunt had come to her rescue.

"Two cheeseburgers, coming right up." André went off to put the order in with the chef. He brought back a cup of coffee for Lela and a cherry phosphate for Diana.

"Thank you," they said in unison.

Moments later, he returned with their food and placed it on the counter in front of them. "There's a Cary Grant film playing at the BigTime Cinema and a Humphrey Bogart film at the ShowHouse. Which will it be?"

"Diana, which would you like to see?" Lela felt she should leave the decision up to her niece. After all, she was the reason André had asked them to go in the first place.

"I'd like to see Cary Grant's new movie, 'Penny Serenade.'" Diana said, then took a bite out of her cheeseburger.

"Great. I'll pick you both up at 7:00 on Saturday. We'll see a movie then have a bite to eat afterwards."

"What fun!" Lela said excitedly, hoping Diana would join in enthusiastically.

"That would be wonderful, André. Thank you." Diana's voice was calm, cool, and smooth, however it did not hinder André's enthusiasm.

"Great, " he replied, then excused himself so that he could acknowledge a party of four people that had just come in to the café.

"Oh, Diana, I'm so excited. We're going to go to the movies in an automobile," Lela exclaimed in an excited whisper after André had walked away.

"Yes, that sounds like fun." Diana didn't mean a word of what she was saying, and Lela could sense it.

"I know it's been hard for you today, but later on you'll really appreciate what André has done for us and what he can do for us in the future." Lela turned to eat her food, missing the glaring look that Diana gave her.

છ

On Saturday night, André pulled up in front of Lela's flat in his 1941 Packard 110, deluxe four-door sedan. Its sleek black body was shiny clean, the inside sported black leather seats that had been treated with leather conditioner giving the car a clean, masculine smell.

André was dressed in a pair of pleated black trousers, white button down short-sleeved shirt with a tie, and black wing-tip shoes that were freshly polished. His dark hair was combed back neatly and held in place with hair tonic. In his hands he carried a large bouquet of flowers.

Knocking confidently on the door, he was greeted by Diana. "André, please come in," she gestured with a sweep of her arm.

"These are for you, Diana." He held the bouquet of flowers out to her, and experienced a fleeting moment of trepidation. What if she didn't like them?

Taking them into her arms, she fussed, "They're beautiful! They smell wonderful, too. Thank you, André."

He smiled in acknowledgement, relieved that she was so delighted. A beautiful mixture of purple, yellow, white, and pink wildflowers, André had personally directed the florist in putting the arrangement together.

"I'll go put them in water," Diana turned, and the full skirt of her dress flared out teasingly as she did.

Lela had been putting the finishing touches on her hair and came out to see what the fuss was all about. "Oh, Diana, the flowers are beautiful! Here, let me help you with them."

Taking the bouquet, she went to the kitchen cupboard and pulled out a cut glass vase that was barely large enough for the oversized bouquet.

"Did you have to get such a large bouquet, André? I mean I practically have to stuff the flowers into the vase." Lela gave André a sidelong glance of approval.

"I'll make sure to bring them in a vase next time." He said, good-naturedly indicating that there *would* be a next time, or so he hoped.

"Well, if we're all ready to go..." Lela decided she'd have to appoint herself the leader for the evening since Diana was behaving shyly, and André was obviously too smitten to think properly.

Holding the door open, she waited for Diana and André to make their way down the stairs, then closed and locked the door behind her.

André held the rear, driver's side door open for Lela, and held out his hand for her to use as support as she stepped into the car. Next, he walked Diana around to the passenger's side, opened the door and helped her into the car. Taking the driver's seat, he started the engine and they were on their way.

"Your car is gorgeous!" Lela said excitedly from the back seat.

"Not as gorgeous as the passengers," André said. With his usual self-assurance, he smiled at Diana. Lela noticed, with relief, that Diana returned the smile.

"How often did you go in and help your father at his café in Greece?" André asked, glancing briefly over at Diana, then turning his attention back to the road.

"I always went in on Saturday mornings and sometimes after school to help serve orders and clean tables."

"Did you enjoy your work, or was it out of obligation that you went?

"Oh, I loved talking to the people who came in. I felt as though I were entertaining friends in my very own dining room."

André gave an understanding nod. "Yes, that's how I feel about my café. I know many of my customers personally."

"You mean I'm not the only one whose order you know by heart?" Lela pretended to sound crushed.

"You and Diana have become very special to me these past few months. It's not often that I spend time with my female customers outside of the café."

"If it's not too personal, why haven't you married yet?" Diana asked, as Lela cringed inwardly at the question. Why did her niece have to be so bold and ask such a potentially embarrassing question?

André was unaffected. "It's not too personal. I've simply not had the time. I've been far too busy establishing myself here in America to find a wife. Besides, the women that I've met so far have been unimpressive." His appreciative look at Diana held a spark of hope.

The past several days had changed Diana from a lovesick, homesick, hopeful child to a woman facing the harsh realities of life in a different country. She had recovered quickly from the news about Nikoli, almost too quickly. For five entire months, she had held on to the hope that Nikoli was going to come to America and find her. Now that she knew that would never happen, what could she do? What were her choices?

One of her choices was sitting beside her, she realized. Diana could feel André's eyes on her every so often as his attention was torn between his driving and looking at her.

The remainder of the evening went by smoothly. The BigTime Cinema was packed with others anxious to see Cary Grant's new movie. Afterwards, André took both women out to a malt shop where they had ice cream sundaes.

Back at the apartment, André bid farewell. "Thank you, both, for such a pleasant evening. I hope you enjoyed yourselves as much as I did." His eyes lingered on Diana.

"We had a ball, didn't we?" Lela said a little too anxiously, turning to Diana.

"Yes, thank you. It was very kind of you to show us such a good time."

She'd really had a good time, too. André had been a gentleman all evening, never failing to pay for anything, open a door for her and Lela, or say a kind word.

"Would it be too forward, then, for me to ask you both out again for next Saturday?" He had seen his opportunity, and he wasn't going to pass it up.

"We'd love it!" Lela said, almost too quickly.

André turned to Diana, awaiting her answer. "That would be fine." Diana replied, although without the enthusiasm of Lela. André, however was undaunted by Diana's seeming lack of excitement

"I'll see you, as usual, when you come into the café for your Friday night meal. If you care to come during the middle of the week, it'll be my treat." It was becoming difficult for André to hide his eagerness. He knew that the evening had come to an end, but he didn't want to leave.

Lela sensed André's predicament, and before he could continue his rambling and make a fool out of himself, she said, "We'll come by during the week, André, thanks for the offer. I'll walk you to the door."

He was already standing near the door, next to Diana, but had momentarily lost his senses. "Oh, right. Thanks."

"Good night," Diana said quietly.

"Good night." For one brief moment, he looked as though he was going to start talking again, but he stopped himself.

"Thanks again, André. We had a swell time." Lela held the door open for him and waved good bye once again as he walked down the stairs.

Shutting the door, then leaning against it, Lela breathed a sigh of relief. "He likes you, Diana. He *really, really* likes you!"

Diana had sunk onto the sofa with her head down. "Oh, what am I supposed to do? I mean, I like André. He's very nice. But I don't have that feeling about him!"

"What do you mean?" Lela stepped away from the door to stand beside her niece.

"You know, the one that ties your stomach up in knots when you look at the man you love. *That* feeling."

"That's not love, Diana. That's lust. There's a big difference between the two."

"Is there? Or do you just want me to believe that so I don't break down again."

"Oh, darling. Of course I don't want you to fall apart. I want you to be happy. Sometimes, in fact most of the time, life just doesn't go our way. We plan, hope, and dream and usually only come to accomplish a fraction of what we want."

Diana was wrapped in a cocoon of anguish. "I loved Nikoli so very much. I loved him with every breath I took and every beat of my heart." She pressed her hand against her mouth to stifle a cry. Would her pain never end?

Lela sat down on the sofa beside Diana, wrapping her arms around the girl. "I understand what you're going through. You'll get over him— you'll definitely get over him! Just give yourself some time."

Diana nodded her head in comprehension and agreement. She would make herself get over Nikoli. He had betrayed her by marrying another woman. Why hadn't he come for her? Why hadn't he gotten aboard a ship and come in search of her?

Yes, she would get over him. But she would never forget him.

CHAPTER FOURTEEN

In Nikoli's absence, Catherine and Jason made Sophia feel at home. All of them carried on their usual, daily activities. Jason's fishing business had slowed down because of the war. Most of the young boys who worked for him had gone away to fight.

Catherine and Sophia did their usual household chores. While shopping at the market, both women were greatly aware of the absence of men. The wives and sisters of the men who had headed for the mainland to defend their country were running the open-air stands.

News had reached Crete of the outcome thus far of the war. The overall somber mood of the people of the island was indicative of the setbacks that the Greek army had suffered. Telegrams were delivered personally to the families of the dead and severely wounded. Whenever Sophia and Catherine saw the delivery boy ride by their house on horseback, each would turn to the other with relief-flooded eyes.

"I have come to despise the sound of horses hooves coming towards us on the road," Sophia said one day as she and Catherine sat mending clothes.

"So have I," Catherine couldn't have agreed more wholeheartedly.

Sophia hadn't told Catherine yet, but she was fairly sure that she was pregnant. Nikoli had to return to help her raise their child. Every morning and every night she prayed that Nikoli would return home safely.

ɷ

On Sunday, April 27, 1941, Germany entered Athens. German soldiers filled the streets wearing their gray uniforms, and with cold, uncaring eyes. All of northern Greece, Crete, and some of the surrounding islands were affected by the occupation. The Greek people had become prisoners in their own homeland.

Now that the fighting was over, the Greek men who had survived would return to their homes. Sophia's heart was filled with fear as the days passed and there was no sign of Nikoli. Surely, he should have returned home by now.

Nearly two weeks later, Catherine and Sophia were preparing a midday meal when there was the sound of approaching hooves. This time, instead of the sound waning into the distance, it stopped outside. Catherine told herself that she hadn't heard correctly. Either the galloping of the horse had continued past their home or it had stopped, perhaps next door. Certainly, the horse and rider had not paused in front of their house.

There was a rapping at the front door. Wearily, Sophia looked over at Catherine, and pulled in a ragged breath. With trembling hands, Catherine set down her knife. Jason was down by the sea fishing and wouldn't be home for lunch yet; besides, he wouldn't have knocked.

Please, oh please, don't let it be the messenger about Nikoli. Sophia chanted over and over in her mind as she and Catherine, arm in arm, went to see who was at the door.

It must have taken the women too long because the caller impatiently rapped against the door again, this time harder and louder

Catherine looked at Sophia with eyes that said, 'You open the door, I haven't the courage'. In slow motion, Sophia reached her hand out to release the latch.

A young boy, no more than 15, stood before them. He was dressed in dusty dark pants, black riding boots, a white cotton shirt, and a mail pouch was slung across his chest. In his hand was a white envelope, which he held out towards Sophia. "I have a special delivery addressed to Sophia, Jason, and Catherine Agorinos."

Neither woman could find their voice to speak, and both were paralyzed with fear. The delivery boy looked inquisitively at the women then held the envelope out towards them even further, waiting for one of them to take it from him. There was no compassion in his dark eyes. He was simply doing his job.

Catherine found the strength to take the envelope from his hand, and the moment she did so, the young boy quickly turned and hurried back to his horse. He had learned from past experience that it was best for the messenger of bad news to be long gone when the seal of the envelope had been torn open.

Wordlessly, and with unsteady hands, Catherine used a letter opener to cleanly tear the top edge of the envelope and remove the letter. But before she could read its contents, Jason appeared in the doorway.

"I just passed the messenger boy on my way home for lunch." His eyes held the unspoken question, *did he stop here?* Catherine and Sophia didn't have to say anything for him to know the answer.

"If I don't read the letter, we can still pretend that he is alive and well and returning home to us." Catherine said in a wavering voice.

Jason took three long strides towards his wife and put his strong arms around her.

"I will read the letter to myself and then you can believe whatever you want to." He didn't want to lose his son and his wife all in one day. If it meant holding on to her sanity by pretending that Nikoli was still alive, then Jason would accept that. It would be much more difficult if she were to lapse into an inconsolable grief.

Kissing the top of Catherine's head, Jason released her and took the letter from her hand. Unfolding the single sheet of paper, he began to read.

Echoes in the Hallway

To Sophia, Jason and Catherine Agorinos, the wife and parents of Nikoli Agorinos.

Let it be known that on April 18,1941, Nikoli Agorinos bravely and valiantly fought against the German and Italian armies in order to protect our beloved homeland of Greece.

It is with honor that he died and we hope that in your grief you will remember the greater purpose of his death.

With deep regret,
The Grecian Army

His son was dead. The boy whom he had loved and cherished and raised into a young man, would never fish with him again. Jason fell to his knees, the paper falling to the floor with him, and from his mouth came the most wretched sound. His bereavement tore at his soul as if the flesh were being ripped away from his body. It was he who had become inconsolable.

Catherine went to her husband and knelt beside him. They clung to one another, rocking back and forth in agony.

Sophia stood in the center of the room, watching them for a moment, then wrapping her arms around herself she joined them with her tears. Nikoli was not coming home. He would never hold her in his arms again, and he would never see his unborn child. It was that thought, most of all, that pushed her over the edge of sanity.

CHAPTER FIFTEEN

On December 7, 1941, the bombing of Pearl Harbor officially marked the United State's entry into World War II. The entire country would experience great changes because of the war. Women were forced to join the work force, many working in steel factories in order to maintain the production needed for the war effort.

Within her first year in America, Diana's entire life had changed drastically. After their wedding in November of 1941, André had moved Diana and Lela out of their small flat and into his beautiful home on Chicago's more fashionable north side.

Built of dark red brick with wood trim painted white, the house flaunted a wooden wrap-around front porch and dark solid oak front doors which opened up into a marble foyer complete with a crystal chandelier. A winding staircase led to a second level, which had four bedrooms.

The first floor consisted of a library/den, a sitting room for receiving guests, and a full-size kitchen with a walk-in pantry. André had hired an architect to design the house for him, which was almost a complete replica of a full-size mansion he had seen in a movie.

This home was André's mark of prosperity to the world. Not only had he made a success of his restaurant, he had used the profits from that business to obtain parcels of land in the Chicago area which he planned to either develop or sell for a tidy profit in the future.

Diana and Lela happily went about redecorating the house, giving it a distinct air of femininity. They had resigned from their duties at the Johnson household in order to devote their time to taking care of André and his home, and to help him at the café.

André had made no secret of the fact that he desired children. He needed someone to leave his legacy to. His children would be born and raised in this great land of opportunity. For even with America at war, the Café Skyros continued to flourish, and he was certain that one day the land he had purchased would make him and his family wealthy beyond his wildest imaginings.

"Auntie Lela, we need to get going. It's almost the lunch hour and I told André we'd be there to help him."

It was nearly Christmas and the café had been busier than usual with people stopping by for a cup of coffee after shopping. The dinner crowd was larger because many of the women who now worked preferred to eat out after a long day. André was considering opening up another location and having Lela and Diana help him run it.

"How many times have I told you, you don't have to call me Auntie? Just plain Lela is fine! Especially now that we're working together at the café, it sounds more professional."

"I know, but it's hard for me *not* to call you Auntie." Then pausing and smiling she said, "Lela, we have to go."

"That's much better. I only need to put my coat and boots on and I'm ready."

Lela kicked off her house slippers and stepped into her boots. After putting on her warm winter coat, she grabbed a canvas bag that held her work shoes.

Instead of the old coat that Lela had given her a year ago, Diana was wearing a brand new full-length fur coat that André had given to her as a wedding gift.

André had proposed to buy Diana a car and teach her how to drive, but she had declined. He had then offered to come by and pick Lela and Diana up and bring them to the café, but Diana didn't want him to leave his customers. Instead, the women walked the few blocks to the café.

"I thought it would be nice to put up some Christmas decorations at the café. Do you think André would mind?" Diana asked.

"I think he'd love the idea. Why don't you and I pick up some garland at Woolworth's on the way?"

"Okay! We can put it up when it gets slow between lunch and dinner."

When they reached the café with their purchases, André was more than pleased with the idea. "I knew you would be the best thing that ever happened in my life. Not only are you beautiful and hard working, but you're smart too! I needed a woman's touch around here. I've never put up Christmas decorations in the past, but it would be an especially good idea this year, now that we're at war. People need to be able to have somewhere to go that's familiar and comforting."

Diana agreed. "I think so too. Lela and I will put up the decorations after the lunch crowd settles down."

André kissed her tenderly on the cheek. "Thank you, Diana."

She smiled at him and moved away to put on her work apron and shoes. As usual, the lunch crowd was in a hurry. With Diana and Lela helping out, André was able to serve more people with more efficiency, which resulted in additional profits.

After the final lunch table had been cleared and wiped off, Diana and Lela went about decorating the café. Red and green garland was hung around the entire room. The front door was framed with silver garland. Diana had purchased several boxes of red and white candy canes, which she arranged in a drinking glass near the register.

"Make sure you give a candy cane to each patron as they pay their bill," she instructed André and Lela.

André looked around the café approvingly. "You've done a great job. Thank you."

"It was fun! I have one other request to make, though."

André looked at Diana in anticipation. She never ceased to amaze him with her talents. "What would that be?"

"Change the radio station. The music you have playing now is… well, let's just say that it's old fashioned."

"Old fashioned?" André pretended to be hurt.

"Oh, I didn't mean to hurt your feelings, but I think if you had something a little more upbeat playing that it would make the atmosphere more appealing."

"Diana, I trust you completely. Since you and Lela have been working here with me, I've been able to turn over more tables. If you say we must change the radio station, then we will. I'll let you choose a new one."

He showed her where the main radio control was in the back office of the café. She found a station that she knew played more of the modern songs she enjoyed. Currently, a Christmas carol was on the air.

"If we get any busier, I'll be forced to open another location!"

"Lela and I are prepared to help you if that's what you want." Diana said, matter-of-factly.

A faintly eager look flashed in André's eyes. "What I'd really like is for you and I to have a child together. I want that more than I want another café."

They were alone in his office where he had taken her to change the radio station.

It was a small room with a desk, two metal filing cabinets, and a two-seater sofa where André would sometimes nap instead of going home, before he'd met Diana.

Diana quivered when he touched her arm, his words causing a tremor to course through her. "André, I…"

He quieted her with his lips, folding her into his arms drawing her against himself.

She tried to protest. "What if someone comes in?"

André moved over to the door and locked it, never taking his eyes off Diana. Returning to where she was standing, his hands began a lustful exploration of her body, pulling her soft luscious curves against his male hardness. He stroked the smooth lines of her back, waist, and hips until she softened under his touch.

André had always been gentle with Diana. On their wedding night he had made sure that she was comfortable in every way before attempting to make love to her. Candles had been lit, wine poured into crystal glasses, and he had even sprayed the bed linens with a soft romantic scent. Diana had been sweetly surprised that night and as a result, had never been afraid of his touch.

Here in his office, he felt a demanding arousal. Breathlessly, he led Diana to the sofa and eased her downward. She felt her awakened response and let out a small cry. Not bothering to fully undress her or himself, André impatiently succumbed to his need.

André held onto Diana, burying his face in her breasts. "Diana, I don't know what came over me." He looked up into her face, her cheeks shiny with tears.

"How can I go back to work now? Everyone will know! I'll be so embarrassed." Diana closed her eyes feeling utterly miserable.

Relieved to know that this was all she was upset about, André let out a chuckle,

"Let me help you pull yourself together." Helping her to her feet, he smoothed out her skirt, buttoned up the front of her shirt and tucked it back in place. Taking a comb from his back pocket, he rearranged Diana's hair, which she'd had pulled back and held in place with a clip.

Standing back a step to look her over, he smiled lovingly at her. "There now, you look just as you did before coming back here to change the radio station. Let me see you smile."

Obediently, Diana smiled at him. It was impossible to be angry with him about anything. He was very kind to her and Lela, and because of him she had a beautiful home and a secure future. If only she could love him the way she had loved Nikoli.

"Thank you, André."

"No, Diana, thank *you* for that unexpected pleasure in the middle of my day!"

Opening the office door, they walked out to the front of the café where Lela was taking a customer's order.

CHAPTER SIXTEEN

"You will fish for my men, now. Every day, you will bring me your catch and I will give you one tenth of it as your pay. The more you catch, the more you will be able to keep for yourself and for your friends." The German officer spoke to Jason in clipped, broken English, the only language common to both of them.

The Germans were rationing everything from water and bread to firewood. The elderly were dying from disease and starvation and children suffered from severe malnutrition.

Every night, Jason took out his fishing boat with the help of some of the older men who had not gone to fight the war. And now, every morning, Jason would present his catch to the German officer who would then portion off what he considered to be a tenth. Jason would place his portion into a bucket and take it home with him.

The fish were then divided amongst the men who had helped him. They in turn would bring it home to their families and sometimes share what they could with friends and neighbors.

Small groups of resistance fighters had formed. Nails were scattered onto roads causing German jeep and truck tires to blow out. Messages were painted on the walls of buildings with oil paints that read, "**GIVE US FOOD.**" The war had touched all of their lives, changing them forever.

Those who had sent their children to America prior to the war held on to the knowledge and hope that at least someone in their family would survive. Diana's father continued his work at the café, however it was German soldiers that he served, and he didn't take in pay for his work. The only form of retribution he received was food, which was enough for anyone given the circumstances.

Many times, Isadora and Constantine Persephonus wished they had accompanied their daughter on her trip to America. Had they known the war would have come to this, they would have fled for their lives. They had received letters from Diana and knew that she was doing well, much to their great relief.

One day, while Constantine was preparing lunch for the soldiers, he was distracted by a barely audible knock on the back door of his kitchen. Opening up the door, he looked down to see a pathetically thin child with his hands held out. "Please...food." The child's voice was weak.

Looking up and down the alley to make sure that there were no soldiers about, Constantine quickly ushered the child inside. With a ladle, he filled a wooden bowl with soup and handed it to the child who was crouched in the corner by the stove. Eagerly, he slurped the still-hot soup until it was completely gone and then proceeded to lick the inside of the bowl.

Constantine looked away in horror. His people were starving and here he was forced to serve food to the Germans! Anger caused his temples to pulsate. He spoke to the boy in a hushed voice, "I want you to come here every day for a bowl of soup, do you hear me? But you mustn't tell anyone or we'll both be in great danger!"

The boy nodded his head 'yes' eagerly, gratefully, in agreement. Then, Constantine opened the back door, and after making sure it was safe he ushered the boy back out into the alley.

On December 28, 1941, Sophia gave birth to a healthy baby boy. It had been a long and difficult labor and Catherine had stayed by her side the entire time with the midwife.

Wiping Sophia's brow with a soft cloth, Catherine looked down at the newborn baby, which the midwife had placed in Sophia's arms. "He's beautiful. He reminds me of…" Her voice trailed off and caught in a sob.

Sophia looked up at her mother-in-law with tears of her own, "Let's name him Nicholas in honor of his father."

Catherine smiled gratefully at the young woman who had become a daughter to her. "Thank you, my dear."

For the next week, Catherine helped Sophia recover from the delivery. She did everything except feed the baby. It was a difficult time for anyone to have a child, but Catherine found caring for little Nicholas a welcome distraction.

One day, as part of his pay, Jason brought home an entire loaf of German bread. Catherine excitedly cut off a large piece for Sophia and served it to her on a plate.

Sophia was propped up with pillows on the sofa and appreciatively took the plate from Catherine. "Thank you. I feel like a queen!"

"It's been a wonderful week. I'm glad to have something to do and keep my mind off of them," she nodded her head in the direction of the street where German soldiers made their daily rounds.

"Has there been any news?"

"No, things are going to get worse before they get better. They are rounding up the Jews and having them check in every day at a designated area."

"Whatever for?"

"I hear that they have been doing terrible things to them. It's only a matter of time before they will be taken by train to a camp." Catherine's voice trailed off. Hopefully, they were just rumors. No one could be so cruel as to try and eliminate an entire race of people, could they?

Sophia fell silent, the bread uneaten on the plate in front of her. "Sometimes, it all seems too much to bear."

The baby started to cry and Catherine went quickly over to him. Jason had built a square box out of scrap wood, and Catherine had made a mattress out of left over material and goose feathers to complete the makeshift crib for Nicholas.

"There, there, little one. Mama's right here." Catherine carried the baby over to Sophia who took him into her arms.

On October 12, 1944, Greece was liberated from North to South. Four long years had passed since the Greek army had victoriously defended their border against the Italians. And for three and one half years, the Greek people had endured the occupation of the German army on their soil.

During the Occupation, many Greek people had died of starvation, malnutrition, and disease. Greek Jews had been rounded up and taken away by the trainload, never to be seen again. The lucky ones were those who had friends in the resistance and were hidden away in the rocky hills of the Greek countryside. Some had gone for months without ever seeing the light of day for fear of being captured.

Because Jason had been able to bring food home for his family, baby Nicholas had grown to be a healthy three-year old boy. Everyone in the household adored him because of his sunny disposition.

Only weeks before the end of the war and Germany's exit from Greece, Isadora and Constantine Persephonus had been shot to death in the middle of the town square as an example of what happened to those who disobeyed the orders of the German army.

Constantine had been able to feed the little boy who had come begging at the back door of the café. On one occasion, they had not been careful enough and Constantine had been found out. He and his wife were forced from their beds at gunpoint, driven into town, and shot in front of a firing squad.

It would be months before Diana would receive any news of this incident. Throughout the entire Occupation, all mail coming in or going out was censored. The last letter that Diana had received from her parents had been months ago with large portions of it blacked out.

Diana had written to her parents to tell them of the birth of her daughter, Alexis Stephanos on September 2, 1942. And in August of 1944 she had written to tell them of the birth of her son, André Stephanos II.

With the ending of the war in October of 1944, Diana was looking forward to the possibility of her parents moving to America and meeting their grandchildren for the first time. They would be so happy to see that their daughter had become a prosperous part of the American dream.

PART II

CHAPTER SEVENTEEN

CHICAGO, September 1972

Alexis Stephanos sat at her desk staring at the blue prints in front of her. The plans for the new mall were coming along smoothly. The parcel of land that her father had left to her in his will was the perfect location. Now, all she had to do was meet personally with the architect and get the project under way. If all went well, the new mall would be completed within the year. Just in time for the holiday rush.

With a freshly manicured finger, Alexis pressed the button of her intercom. "Beth, has my appointment today with Mr. Agorinos been confirmed?"

"Yes, it has Alex," Beth referred to her boss by her nickname. "He should be here in about ten minutes."

"Please make sure that there's a fresh pot of coffee for our meeting, would you?"

"Sure, no problem."

As a woman in predominantly a man's business, Alexis had found that it worked best to refer to herself as Alex. Tall and slender as her mother and grandmother had been, Alexis found that high heels helped her create an imposing image to the men she had to deal with on a daily basis. Her business suits were always of a dark color—navy blue, black, and sometimes burgundy with skirts that fell slightly above her knee.

With the free-love movement of the 60's behind her, it was now even more important for Alexis to prove her business expertise. Throughout college, she'd had to endure being the only girl in most of her architectural and business classes. After graduation, she and her father, André Stephanos, had formed a partnership in which they had personally overseen the development of some of the property he had acquired over the years.

Upon André's death, he had left the remainder of his property holdings to Alexis. His son, Andrew Stephanos, had taken over his chain of restaurants, and was successfully running them. He and his sister had a wonderful relationship and each reveled in the other's prosperity.

Alex and Andrew took turns having dinner with their mother and their great-aunt, Lela, who looked after Diana, now that their father was gone.

Diana had slipped into a world of her own when the news of her parent's demise had reached her, months after the war had ended. From that day forward, her children would never really know their mother, who was now a shadow of her former self. Alexis had been a little over two years old and Andrew only 7 months old. Lela had taken over the care of the children, and by the time Alexis was seven, she had taken it upon herself to look after her younger brother. They had become, and still were, inseparable.

Alexis made sure that she had all of her notes ready for her meeting. Pulling out a small mirror from her desk drawer, she applied a fresh coat of rose-colored lipstick and brushed her long, dark, perfectly straight hair to a smooth shine.

When the buzzer sounded, she instructed Beth to have Mr. Agorinos come into her office. Alexis was standing at her desk to greet him. "Good afternoon, please have a seat."

Nick Agorinos sat down in one of the two chairs that were situated in front of Alexis's desk. He was dressed in a dark gray, pin-stripe suit. His white dress shirt was crisply pressed and accented with a dark burgundy tie.

Alex was immediately taken aback by how handsome he was. She also became instantly aware of his air of self-confidence.

At the same time as Alexis was making her appraisal of Nick, he was appreciatively taking in her long slender legs and shapely figure. He had to remind himself that he was here for a business meeting.

"Would you like a cup of coffee?" Alexis asked.

"Sure, black would be fine."

Alexis pressed the intercom and asked Beth to bring in two cups of coffee.

"I've reviewed the blue prints, Mr. Agorinos. I can tell you that I am more than pleased with them."

"Thank you. With the new indoor mall craze, I've been very busy."

"Yes, that's why I was pleased that our company was able to secure you for the job. You have an excellent reputation for being very picky. So have I."

"Excuse me, but when am I going to get to meet Alex Stephanos?"

"Oh, pardon me. I didn't properly introduce myself to you did I?"

Nick shook his head.

Holding out her hand to him from across the desk, Alexis said, "I'm Alexis Stephanos, but most people refer to me as Alex."

Nick had stood to shake the hand she offered, but paused on his way to sitting back down in his chair. Still standing, he asked suspiciously, "*You're* Alex Stephanos?"

"Yes," she said with a satisfied smile.

"I didn't come here to play games. If you're Alex Stephanos, then I'm leaving." Nick straightened his suit coat indignantly.

Confused, Alexis shook her head in bewilderment.

"I don't deal with women in business. They're fickle as all hell and I can't run a smooth operation just because you might get a whim to change the location of all the plug sockets."

"Is that all you think I'm capable of deciding? My father and I have developed property all around the Chicago area. I know the importance of making a good decision and sticking to it, Mr. Agorinos."

"This is a major project. You have bitten off way more than you can chew. A mall is a very huge undertaking."

"That's why I want to hire the very best team of people, which included you."

"Included?"

"Yes, as of this moment you're fired."

"I'm fired?" Nick repeated defensively.

"Yes."

"You can't fire me, I quit." Nick grabbed his brief case and stormed out of Alex's office.

Angry and shaken, Alexis pressed the intercom. "Beth, have my car brought around for me and set up an appointment with my masseuse. I need to get out of here and unwind!"

"Right away, Alex." Beth had been shocked that within minutes of his entering her boss's office, Mr. Agorinos had turned right around and come back out, obviously agitated.

Picking up her phone, Alexis dialed her brother's number at the restaurant where he kept his main office. It was the same office their father had used over the years, but it had been remodeled several times since then. Andrew's secretary answered the phone.

"Is my brother there?" Alexis asked, impatiently.

Immediately recognizing the familiar voice, she answered, "No, he's on his way to the west side location. Should I have him call you later if he calls in for messages?"

"Yes, thank you." Slamming down the phone, Alexis rubbed the bridge of her nose. Without bothering to use the intercom, she yelled out, "Beth, is my car ready yet?"

Gina Becker

Alexis felt the tension melt as the skilled hands of the masseuse smoothed her knotted muscles. "You need to relax, Missy Stephanos," the oriental man said as he worked at rubbing out a particular knot in her neck.

"I know Chan, but can you believe the audacity of someone telling me that they don't want to do the job because they're afraid I'll start moving the plug sockets around?"

"Maybe he like you," Chan replied.

"Likes me? He hated me! He resents my ability to function in a predominantly male field."

Chan shrugged. "Maybe. But I think he like you."

"Ow!" Alexis let out a shrill cry as Chan began working on yet another knot, this time in her right shoulder area.

"You need to relax, Missy Stephanos." Chan repeated as he continued to rub out the sore spot, despite her protests.

ஒ

Upon Alexis's return to her office, Beth gave her the message that Andrew had called with a number where he could be reached.

"Thanks, Beth. I'm going to stay late tonight. You can leave as soon as you're done filing the correspondence for the day."

"Okay. I'll see you tomorrow."

Alexis dialed Andrew's number. "Andrew Stephanos," he answered.

"Hey little brother. How's it goin'?"

"Alex, what's up?"

"Oh, I just called to tell you about my terrible day."

"What happened? Do I need to take someone for a ride down to the river in the trunk of my car?"

Alexis laughed at her brother's implications of defending her. "No, nothing that serious." She proceeded to tell him about her meeting with Nick Agorinos. "Can you believe he said that to me?"

"Plug sockets, huh? With the kind of money that guy could make off of the project, I'd say that if you wanted to change the plug sockets around he should be happy to do it for you."

"Thanks, Andrew. You always know how to make me feel better. Now I have to start over with another firm."

"I know you'll pull it off. You always do. That mall will still be open in time for the next Christmas shopping season."

"Yeah, I guess. I really wanted Nick, though. He's the best."

"Then find out who's second best and get him."

"That's what I'm going to do. I hope he's not a jerk too."

"By the way, when are you going to mom's again? I was there last night." Andrew asked, changing the subject.

"Oh, I think Aunt Lela is expecting me tonight. I better get going so that I can still make it over there." Alexis looked at the gold watch on her wrist.

"Okay. She's not doing so well, so don't be shocked. It seems like she's getting worse. She thought I was dad and started asking me questions about the restaurant as if it were still the 1940's." Andrew had always been more sensitive about his mother's illness than Alexis.

"Thanks for the warning. I love you, Andrew."

"Love you too, sis."

Alexis hurriedly hung up the phone and began an eager search of other architectural firms. The one mall that she had admired most was the work of Nick Agorinos. Her next favorite mall had been the work of a man that Alexis knew very little about, Daniel Blake. She made a note to call him in the morning and set up an appointment.

Grabbing her purse and turning the office lights out, Alexis let herself out of the building.

CHAPTER EIGHTEEN

Alexis pulled her BMW 530i into the driveway of her mother's home. Very little had changed since her father's death two years prior. André's death had come as a shock to everyone. Still vibrant and full of energy, he had suffered a fatal heart attack at the still-young age of 58.

When Diana had received the letter about her parent's death, she had become emotionally and mentally unreachable. André had taken over the care of the children with the help of Lela. As a result, both children were much closer with their father, although they both resisted becoming too close with their great aunt because they instinctually felt it would be disloyal to their mother.

Diana's state of mind had become even worse after the death of André. Lela often found Diana wandering around the house talking to imaginary people. Sometimes Diana would talk to people whom Lela had known such as her sister, Isadora, and Constantine, and other times to people whom she had known back in her hometown village in Greece.

Alexis missed her father terribly. He had been the greatest source of strength and joy in her life. She was grateful to him for raising her as he had. André had always been confident in Alexis's ability to work in a man's world. They had worked well together and had developed some of the most upscale property in the Chicago area. André had taken great care to have a will made out earlier in his life so that there wouldn't be a question as to his wishes. It was agreed upon before his death that Alexis would take over the building company and Andrew would take over the management and growth of the restaurants.

Now that André was gone, Alexis and Andrew were each other's mentors. He would often run ideas by Alexis such as remodeling, opening up a new location, and even changes in the menu. Alexis often drew upon Andrew's market awareness and asked his advice for new development projects. After André's death, Alexis had used company profits to purchase more property to develop in the future.

Alexis picked up the large bouquet of fresh cut flowers from the front seat of her car and walked up the pathway to the front door. After ringing the doorbell, she let herself inside.

"Darling!" Lela came towards her with arms open. She had become an eccentric old maid and was wearing a long, flowing dress. The skirt swirled around her ankles as she walked. The dark fabric had geometric patterns on it giving the outfit a busy look. At least a dozen gold and silver bangle bracelets clanked together whenever Lela moved her arms. Her hair, which was kept dark with monthly beauty shop appointments, was swept up into a beehive hairdo and long, gold earrings dangled against her neck.

"Hello, Aunt Lela. How are you?" Alexis hugged her aunt affectionately with the bouquet of flowers still in her hand.

"Oh my, things have been hectic around here." Lela held Alexis at arm's length while keeping her hands on Alexis's shoulders.

"I know. Andrew told me."

"Poor dear. She thought Andrew was your father and started talking to him about changing the radio station in the restaurant. That was ages ago! I was there when she and your father *had* that conversation!"

"If things get bad, maybe we should consider putting her in an extensive care facility."

"Nonsense! I won't hear of it. As long as you and your brother continue to help me financially, I will attend to her myself. Who knows what kind of care she'll get in one of those places. I've heard terrible stories about them."

"Well, I just don't want it to be too much of a burden on you. Thank you for being so loyal to my mother. She's very lucky to have such a caring member of the family."

Lela waved away Alexis's praise. "Besides you and your brother, who else is there for me to look after. Your mother and father were very good to me. It's the least I can do."

Alexis held out the bouquet of flowers to her aunt.

"Oh, you're so thoughtful. Thank you, dear." Lela took the bouquet of flowers from Alexis. "Let's go into the kitchen so I can put these in a vase, and check on dinner, too."

"Where's mother?"

"She's…in there." Lela hesitantly indicated the sitting room with her eyes. Then, uneasily, she walked towards the room with Alexis following her. As the two women drew near the room, they could hear the sound of Diana's voice. She was talking to herself again.

"No, I won't go!"

"But you have to. It's the best thing for you."

"Please, I have to stay and wait for Nikoli!"

"I will not have you talking to your mother that way"

Alexis watched as her mother carried on a full conversation with herself. Goose bumps prickled the back of her neck and along her arms. It was the strangest thing to see her mother sitting in a chair acting out the role of two other people.

"Diana." Lela called out. When Diana did not respond, Lela said her name again, only much louder. "Diana!"

Diana turned towards the sound of Lela's voice. "Is someone there?"

"Mama, it's me. Alexis."

"Who?"

"Your daughter, Alexis."

"I have a daughter? Don't be silly, I'm not old enough to have a daughter."

"Well, then. I would just like to come by and give you a kiss on the cheek to say hello. Would that be okay?"

"I suppose." Diana drew her eyebrows together in uncertainty.

Alexis slowly drew near her mother and as she did, noticed that she smelled clean and sweet. Lela took great care in making sure that Diana bathed every day. After giving her mother a quick peck on the cheek, she kneeled down by the chair in which she was sitting.

"Now, who did you say you were?"

"I'm Alexis. I'm your daughter and you're my mother."

"Is that so? Well, now. I was just saying that I didn't want to leave my home, but my father is making me. Is your father making you leave your home?"

"No, he isn't. Are you hungry?"

"I'm not sure. I'll think about it."

"Okay. I'll come back and get you when the food's ready."

"That's very kind of you."

Alexis lovingly stroked her mother's arm once before turning back to go to the kitchen with her aunt.

Once they were in the kitchen, Lela went into the walk-in pantry to find a vase for the flowers.

"It's so strange to see her talking to herself."

"It's the echoes…" Lela paused in arranging the flowers to look at her great-niece, who was staring at her curiously.

"The what?"

"The echoes in the hallway of her mind. She's responding to the voices she hears in her head. Memories of another time."

"Oh. I've never heard it put quite that way, Aunt Lela."

Lela continued arranging the flowers in the vase as she talked. "Well, I suppose there's a proper, medical term for your mother's condition. But your father insisted on taking care of her himself and wouldn't take her to a doctor."

"Yes, I'm sure there is a proper medical name for it. For the most part, though, I doubt if there's a cure. I would have read about it somewhere. I know there are support groups for those who take care of the mentally disabled."

"Mentally disabled is just a nice way of saying 'crazy', isn't it?"

"I'd hate to think of my mother as crazy."

"Well, it's nothing to be ashamed of. Lots of people are crazy, they just haven't reached the point your mother has yet. I'm just glad that she's still pleasant to be around." Finished arranging the flowers, Lela made her way to the stove where she took the lid off of a large, stainless steel pot. The steam released a tantalizing aroma into the air.

"That smells delicious! Is it your famous Greek stew?"

"Yes, I know it's one of your favorites. With that new mall project coming up I want to make sure you take time to eat right."

"Speaking of the new mall project, I had the worst day." Alexis proceeded to tell Lela about her meeting with Nick. "It's days like today that I really, *really* miss my dad."

"We all miss him very much, darling. He was a strong and decent man and we were all blessed for having known him."

"Yes, we were." Alexis took a seat at the table that was already set with silverware, napkins, two bowls and plates, and two crystal wineglasses. "Is the wine in the refrigerator?"

"Yes, would you mind serving it?"

"Not at all." Alexis got up from her chair and went over to the refrigerator.

Removing the bottle of Greek wine, she pulled the cork and poured a full glass of the claret liquid for each of them.

"I see you need to unwind tonight," Lela smiled, indicating the full wineglasses.

"Yes, I think we *both* do." Alexis returned the smile.

৯৹

That night, Alexis lay in her bed going over the day's events. All things considered, it had been an extremely trying day. First the incident with Nick Agorinos and then the realization that her mother was slipping further and further away from reality—she hadn't even recognized her own daughter!

Frustrated with trying to slow down her mind enough to sleep and finding she was unable to, Alexis went to the kitchen to have a hot cup of herbal tea. Impatiently, she tapped her finger on the counter as the microwave heated the water. The microwave oven was the latest modern invention and the most recent addition to her kitchen. When the bell rang, she placed the teabag in the hot water, carried the mug to the table, and sat down while waiting for it to steep.

Her thoughts immediately turned back to her meeting that day. She had to win Nick Agorinos back on the job! There was no one else in the Chicago area more capable of overseeing a project than he was. His reputation for being a perfectionist was well deserved. Nick paid attention to detail and he took pride in seeing that the blueprints he and his team drew up were executed to the very final aspect.

Besides, he was incredible to look at! He had the darkest brown eyes she'd ever seen, and a head full of thick, dark hair. It had been months since she'd met a man that had captured her attention the way Nick had today. Not only was he good looking, he was self-confident, a trait she found incredibly sexy. However, she reminded herself, he had been a little too self-confident. The very trait, which she found so appealing, had actually worked against her.

That thought threw Alexis right back where she'd started. There was no way any man was going to refer to her as fickle! She didn't need Nick, there were plenty of other wonderful architects who'd be happy to do the job, even if the project was being headed by a woman. She'd build the greatest, most beautiful and popular mall in town. Nick Agorinos would wish he hadn't been so pompous!

Sipping at the hot tea, Alexis let her thoughts whirl about her, something she rarely allowed herself to do. Most of the time, she had to be in such control that there was no room in her day for such rampant speculation.

There was her mother's condition to think about as well. Maybe she and Andrew should make arrangements for her to be evaluated by a physician. Alexis was fairly sure her mother suffered from some form of dementia. With a more accurate diagnosis, perhaps there was something that could be done to help her. There was still so much that was unknown about mental illness, yet many people suffered from it.

Deciding she was finally tired enough to try and sleep again, Alexis took the half-emptied mug to the kitchen sink. Looking at the stack of dishes she'd let pile up during the week, she reminded herself that her housekeeper, Lois, was due to come over tomorrow. Usually, Alexis would pick up after herself and load whatever eating utensils she used into the dishwasher. This week had been so hectic and exciting that she hadn't taken the time.

Grabbing the notepad that she left by the kitchen phone, she wrote down the following:

1. Make doctor's appointment for mom.
2. Call Nick Agorinos, try to get him back.
3. Leave extra money for Lois this week!

Alexis put the list down and looked around the beautifully appointed kitchen. Her father had helped design and build this house, and they had gone through the entire building process together.

White Grecian marble covered the floors and counters of the kitchen. André had insisted she have Grecian marble, in honor of his native land. Custom built, solid oak cabinets had been white-washed giving them a French Provincial look. In the center was a cooking island with a built-in range and stainless steel sink with a gooseneck faucet. An entire corner near the window was devoted to plants of varying shapes and sizes, and hanging baskets of ivy had been strategically placed around the room.

Feeling an unexpected pang of sadness, Alexis felt the tears well up in her eyes as she thought of her father. His touch was everywhere in this house. She missed him terribly, especially at times like this. There was so much she was grateful to her father for. She wondered, less seriously now, what he would say about a microwave oven!

With a deep sigh, she left the list on the kitchen counter, turned out the light and went back to her bedroom to try and get some rest. Tomorrow was going to bring another set of challenges, and she needed to be prepared for it.

Now that Alexis had been able to mentally go over her day and write down some notes, sleep came easily to her.

CHAPTER NINETEEN

Nick Agorinos had learned the hard way about dealing with women in business. He had originally started his career in residential architecture and had become frustrated with the many changes that people tended to make when building a home.

How many times had he completed a set of prints for a client only to have them ask for an entire wall to be moved? "My wife wants the kitchen to be larger, so we'd like the laundry room wall moved inward three feet."

Okay, so it wasn't always the woman who wanted changes. Men could be just as indecisive. Maybe he'd let Alexis's good looks rattle him just a touch. He had felt intimidated by her long legs and shapely figure, and those eyes! Where in the world had she gotten such beautiful green eyes with that dark hair? So the woman had looks *and* brains. A dangerous combination, in Nick's opinion.

There were other architects in the area that would be happy to take on the project.

In his opinion, though, he was the best. Alexis had been right about that! Maybe he would give her another chance.

Pressing the intercom button on his phone, he asked his secretary, "Carley, would you please get Miss Stephanos on the phone for me?"

"Sure, Nick."

"Thanks."

Moments later, Nick was talking to Alexis. "Miss Stephanos, I'd like to apologize for my outburst the other day."

"What's the matter Nick, don't you have enough work to keep you busy? You're the last person I'd expected to hear from today. I've already set up a meeting with Daniel Blake, you know the *other* great architect in the Chicago area?"

So, she wasn't going to be nice. "I guess I deserve that. Well, it seems that you're all set then. I'll let you go."

"No, wait! Look, you really ticked me off the other day and I had to get my jab in. I really do have an appointment with Daniel Blake, though."

"He *is* good, but *I'm* better."

"There you go again. You're very self-confident, or should I refer to it as cocky? I already find myself regarding that trait as both a positive and a negative, Nick."

"I can't help it. I grew up in a very loving home where everyone thought I was the greatest thing in the world."

"That kind of thing could lead to therapy. When a kid grows up and finds out that there are other people who are just as good as they are it can cause a nervous breakdown."

"Are you implying that Daniel Blake is just as good as me?"

"Will you promise not to have a nervous breakdown if I say 'yes'?"

"He is *not* as good as me, Alex!"

"That remains to be seen. I'll contact you after I've met with Mr. Blake. Have a nice day." Alexis smiled viciously as she hung up the phone.

Nick's hand was shaking as he slammed the phone down. "I hate that woman!"

Hearing Nick's outburst in the outer office, Carley pressed the intercom button. "Is everything all right in there, Nick?" her voice was laced with concern.

"No! I mean yes. I'll be all right. Thank you for asking." Nick was still frowning as Carley judiciously went back to work.

❧

Alexis wondered how long she should let Nick sweat. She hadn't really made the appointment with Daniel Blake yet. The truth was, Alexis had been on her way to picking up the phone to contact Mr. Blake, when Nick had called.

How dare he be so arrogant! Maybe she really didn't want to work with him after all. Alexis had grown up with confident men. Her father and brother were both sure of their place in this world, but they had never displayed the kind of behavior that Nick Agorinos had.

Suddenly remembering that she had wanted to call around for a doctor to take her mother to, Alexis put Nick out of her mind for the time being. She'd give them both a couple of days to cool off before calling again.

Pulling out her phone book of the Chicago area, Alexis made a methodical search of doctors who specialized in diseases of the elderly. Choosing five doctors whose locale was near her mother's home, Alexis began to call each of the offices. One by one, she eliminated them by the criteria she had established.

"Doctor Harvey's office, could you please hold?"

Before Alexis could reply, she was put on hold, and left there. Using the 'speaker' feature on her phone, she was able to look over her mail while waiting. However, after five minutes of being left waiting, Alexis disconnected the call and crossed the doctor's name off of her list.

The next call was answered by a receptionist who seemed irritated that Alexis was disturbing her busy day and impatiently answered Alexis's questions. Deciding against making an appointment, Alexis thanked the woman and crossed that doctor's name from her list.

It wasn't until her fifth call that Alexis felt she had finally found the right place.

"Good afternoon, doctor William's office, how can I help you?"

"Hi, I'm calling in regards to my mother. I believe she may have Alzheimer's disease, but I'm not sure. Does Doctor Williams treat this particular disease?"

"Yes, he specializes in geriatric medicine, which is the treatment of diseases of the elderly. We have an appointment open tomorrow afternoon at 1:00. Would you like me to put your mother's name down?"

"Sure," Alexis immediately felt at ease with the young woman at the other end of the phone, and gave her the proper spelling of her mother's name.

"Do you know where our office is located?" The receptionist asked.

Alexis indicated the address she'd taken out of the phone book and the receptionist provided more explicit directions, which Alexis wrote down.

"We'll see you tomorrow at 1:00 with your mother. If there are any changes, please call us."

"I will. Thank you." Alexis hung up the phone feeling relieved that she'd finally made the first step in finding help for her mother.

෨

The following day, Alexis picked up her mother for the doctor's appointment.

Diana was not very pleased at first to find out that she was being taken to a doctor's office.

"There's nothing wrong with me. I hate doctors!"

"Mom, please don't make this difficult. I just want to make sure that everything is okay. Will you do it for me?"

Diana looked at Alexis suspiciously for a moment before replying. "All right. I'll go this one time. But just this once, okay?"

"Okay, thanks mom."

Diana turned to hug Lela good-bye, and Alexis gave Lela a look of relief behind her mother's back.

Thankfully, it was a beautiful fall day and Diana seemed to revel in the still warm air. "Oh, I've always appreciated a beautiful sunny day."

"Me too. It makes me feel hopeful about things." Alexis looked over at Diana, who was surprised at the clarity she saw in her mother's eyes. When Diana was in focus, as she was right now, it was hard to understand where her mind wandered to at times.

"Hopeful, that's how I feel today." Without warning, Diana phased out of focus right before Alexis's eyes. "Where did you say we were going?"

"Just for a drive." Discouraged, Alexis didn't bother repeating to her mother that they were on their way to the doctor's office. There was no point in upsetting Diana all over again. Alexis helped her mother out of the car and into the doctor's office. Once Diana was situated in a chair with a magazine, Alexis went to the frosted glass windows to sign in.

A young medical assistant noted Diana's name, then handed Alexis a clipboard. "You'll need to fill out these forms. When you're through, please bring them back up to me."

Alexis returned to sit down next to her mother. She filled out the forms to the best of her knowledge, signed them, and then took them back up to the receptionist.

Ten minutes later, Alexis and Diana were escorted into an examining room to wait for the doctor. Diana was weighed by the assistant, who then wrote the information on her medical chart. She then asked Diana to have a seat on the examination table, and placed a thermometer in her mouth.

"I'm not sick," Diana mumbled around the thermometer.

"I know you're not. It's just for our records to make sure that we've done a thorough evaluation." The receptionist answered patiently. "The doctor will be in shortly."

"I'm not sick," Diana repeated again, reaching to take the thermometer out of her mouth.

"Mom, please…" Alexis got up to put the thermometer back in her mother's mouth just as the doctor walked in.

"Diana Stephanos, it's a pleasure to meet you. I'm doctor Williams." He took Diana's hands between both of his and smiled warmly into her eyes.

Diana was taken aback by his amiable greeting. "Hello. I really don't know why I'm here."

"Well, how about if I ask you a few questions and then we can determine how I can help you." Dr. Williams turned to greet Alexis.

"She wouldn't keep this in her mouth, sorry." Alexis handed him the thermometer.

"That's okay. It's not the most important aspect of this evaluation anyway."

Dr. Williams peered into Diana's eyes and ears. Next, he asked her several questions. Alexis was relieved that her mother was being cooperative so far. That meant she must like the doctor.

Dr. Williams was of medium height and build. In his mid-fifties, he was patient and kind. His dark hair was streaked with gray, and his brown eyes were sympathetic.

Dr. Williams looked at his chart and turned to Alexis. "I understand from my notes that you were concerned that your mother may have Alzheimer's, which is a progressive, neurodegenerative disease. It's usually characterized by memory loss, language deterioration, and poor judgment."

"My mother does have memory loss, but she's still so young. She'll be 50 years old in November of this year."

"Alzheimer's usually strikes after the age of 60." He was checking Diana's blood pressure, peering into her eyes and throat, as he spoke to Alexis. "What are her other symptoms?"

"She forgets what day and year it is. She talks to herself and has conversations with people who have been dead for many years." Alexis told him.

"I've seen that kind of thing before in some of my other patients who have suffered small, repetitive strokes. They're called TIA's, or transient ischemic attacks. The part of the brain that is damaged determines the symptoms. She may have damage in a part of her brain that controls memory. I'd like to run some tests, if you think you can get your mom to cooperate."

Alexis looked warily at her mother. "Mom, Doctor Williams would like to run some tests on you. Do you think that would be okay?"

"I suppose so. He's been so nice." She beamed at the doctor.

Alexis smiled in relief at Diana's willingness to acquiesce.

"You indicated that your mother lives with her aunt."

"Yes, my great-aunt Lela is much older than my mother, but she's very healthy and alert."

"Please let her know that symptoms such as agitation and insomnia can be treated with medication to make the patient more comfortable."

"Of course, I'll be sure to tell her." Alexis was suddenly becoming more aware of the seriousness of her mother's illness. Small strokes could lead to big strokes, which could ultimately lead to paralysis.

"Has your mother ever suffered from stress or depression that you're aware of?"

"What would my mother have to be stressed or depressed about?"

Dr. Williams smiled kindly at Alexis's question. "We only *think* we know our parents. People of your mother's generation were more guarded than we are today. Many of the things we talk about freely were not open for discussion to them." He nodded in the direction of Diana.

Alexis looked at her mother, then at the doctor. In a low, monotone voice she said, "When I was two years old, my mother received a letter from Greece. Her parent's had been shot to death by the German army. Apparently my grandfather, whom I never met, had been feeding a poor Greek boy out of the back of his café. When he was caught, the Germans made an example of him and my grandmother as to what happens to those who disobey orders."

A look of great understanding came into the doctor's eyes. "She was never the same after that, was she?"

Alexis slowly shook her head. "I never really got to know my mother."

"She probably suffered a nervous and emotional breakdown. Some people never get over them."

Alexis nodded her head in agreement. "But you think there's more to her condition than that, don't you?"

"I'm going to order a CAT scan of her head, which you'll have to take your mom to the hospital to have completed. I'll also order some basic blood chemistries. You can take her for those tests today, then I'd like to see her again in about ten days. We can review the results of the tests together at that time. If you have any problems in the interim, please call my office and I'll arrange to see her sooner if necessary."

"Okay, at least we have a starting point which I feel comfortable with."

"Please find out if your mother is getting enough rest at night. It's not unusual for someone in her condition to have insomnia or even wander around at night through a dark house, which could be potentially dangerous."

"I'll ask my Aunt Lela about that when I drop my mother off."

Dr. Williams handed Alexis a prescription slip for a sleeping pill. "If your aunt feels your mother needs these you can fill the prescription."

"Thank you so much. It's been a pleasure meeting you."

Dr. Williams smiled and shook Alexis's hand. Then, turning back to Diana who was lost in thought, he said warmly, "Diana, it was wonderful to meet you."

"Thank you, it was nice to meet you too." Diana said politely, then looked at Dr. Williams blankly as he left the room. Turning to Alexis, she asked, "Who was that?"

"That was Dr. Williams, mom. He said it was time for us to go home now."

"That's nice." Diana followed Alexis out into the waiting room.

The minute Alexis opened the hallway door that led into the lobby, she froze.

What was *he* doing here? Worse yet, her mother was headed right towards him!

"Nikoli?" Diana whispered as she made her way to where Nick was seated with his mother.

Nick Agorinos looked up to see who was addressing him by his father's name.

"My name is Nick, but my father's name was Nikoli. Perhaps you knew him."

Diana was breathing heavily now and tears had formed in her eyes. Her hands had flown up to her mouth in shock.

Alexis came storming over to where they were standing. "Now look what you've done. You've upset my mother!"

"That's not fair. She's the one who came up to me!" Nick's dark eyes flashed angrily at Alexis who was standing behind Diana.

"Nikoli, why did you wait so long to come for me? Do you know how long I've been waiting for you?"

Nick looked at Alexis in bewilderment. "I don't know what she's talking about, I swear. My father's name was Nikoli and she's acting as though she knows me."

"Why are you here?" Alexis asked Nick.

Nick turned towards his mother who was seated next to where he was now standing. "I've been bringing my mother to see Dr. Williams for the past year. She suffers from lapses in memory due to TIA's."

"This was my mother's first visit. She's being evaluated for the same thing."

"Nikoli, why didn't you come sooner?" Diana was insistent.

Alexis came to his rescue. "Mom, this is Nick Agorinos. He's a business associate of mine.

"Did you say Agorinos?"

"Yes, my last name is Agorinos. I came over from the island of Crete with my mother many years ago. My grandparents passed away and my mother and I decided to come to America. I went to school here and started my own architectural firm."

"I grew up in Crete!" Diana said excitedly. "My father had a café there and I used to work for him."

"I never knew my father, he was killed in the war. Everyone says that I look exactly like him."

"Oh, you do! He was a very dear friend of mine and meant the world to me. I was heartbroken when my parents sent me to America. I wrote many letters to Nikoli, but he never wrote back to me."

Turning to his mother, Nick asked, "Mother, do you know who this is?"

Sophia had been sitting very still and quiet in her chair. She made no indication of having heard Diana. When Nick spoke to her, she blinked her eyes uncomprehendingly.

Nick turned back to Alexis and Diana, "I'm sorry, but my mother gets like that sometimes. One minute she seems as coherent as you and I, and then all of a sudden she's unreachable."

Alexis nodded in understanding. "I know what you mean. We've been experiencing the same thing with my mother."

"Maybe we could get together sometime and talk in private, you know, to help each other out." Nick offered

"You seem to be an expert at just about everything," Alexis laughed to hide her annoyance. She had still not forgiven him for the comment he'd made during their meeting.

An uncomfortable silence loomed between them before Nick spoke again. "I was just offering my help."

"I would be so delighted if you would come over to visit me. Please say you will." Diana refused to budge until Nick gave her his word.

Alexis was embarrassed by her mother's enthusiasm. Couldn't she see that she and Nick were not on the best terms right now? No, of course she couldn't.

"I promise. I'll come by to visit you." Nick said. Despite the fact that Alexis was being callous towards him, he didn't feel it was right for him to take it out on Diana.

"This week?" Diana pressed for a firm commitment.

Alexis let out an exasperated sigh and looked expectantly at Nick. "Yes. I'll call Alexis at her office for directions to your home."

Diana let out a squeal of delight. Alexis had never seen her mother so elated before. "Oh, wait until I tell Lela! Thank you." She took Nick's hands between her own and squeezed them.

Alexis had to practically drag her mother away. Looking back one more time, Alexis couldn't help but give Nick a smile of gratitude as she and Diana left the doctor's office.

CHAPTER TWENTY

Andrew and Alexis were sitting in a booth at the north side location of the Café Skyros. "So, what do you think of the remodel job?"

"I love it. Everything looks so modern and welcoming. Dad would be so proud of you." Alexis added wistfully.

"I know. I think about him all the time. Sometimes, I even find myself talking to him, asking him his opinion about things. Do you think I'm crazy?"

"Naw, I do it too." Alexis gave her brother a reassuring smile.

"So what did the doctor have to say about mom?" Andrew took a bite out of his hamburger and waited for Alexis to give him the report.

"Well, he thinks that she may be suffering small, recurrent strokes. I had to take her to the hospital after the office visit for a CAT scan and some blood tests. I'm taking her back to see Doctor Williams in ten days to review the results." Alexis picked up a fork and started toying with her Greek salad.

"I wish there was someone who could tell us exactly what was wrong and then give us some medicine and everything would be okay." Andrew said, then took another bite out of his hamburger.

"I do too. But let's face it—nothing's *that* easy!" Alexis began to eat her salad, temptingly garnished with Greek olives, feta cheese, tomato wedges, and green peppers.

"How's your salad?" Andrew asked.

"Delicious."

"I changed the dressing a little, can you tell?"

"Now that you mention it, it has more flavor than usual."

"It's mint. I added dried mint leaves to the newest batch of dressing."

"It's very good." Alexis said, taking another forkful of salad.

"Thanks," Andrew smiled at his sister. "So, how's old Nicky boy treating you these days?"

"Oh, I almost forgot!" Alexis's hand flew to her forehead. "You wouldn't *believe* who I ran into at the doctor's office."

"Who?"

"Nick Agorinos. And guess what? He and his mother are from the same area of Crete as mom. Mom knew Nick's dad and in fact said that they were very good friends."

"No kidding? That is pretty amazing. Mom remembered all of that?"

"Yes! Oh, Andrew, you should have seen how excited she got when Nick said that he would come over and visit her. I have never seen mom more alive than she was at that moment."

"I'd like to see *that*. Let me know when Nick is going to visit her and I'll come over too. It sounds pretty interesting."

"He's going over to mom's house this Saturday night at 7:00. I'm meeting him there."

"Okay, I'll be there." Andrew took his pocket planner out and wrote the date and time down.

"Nick offered to get together with me and talk about our mothers' condition. He thinks that maybe we can offer support to one another."

Andrew raised his eyebrows, "I'll bet he'd like to offer you his support!"

Alexis waved her hand in disregard, and glared at her brother. "I don't think so."

"Hmm, Alexis Agorinos. That has a certain ring to it."

Alexis picked up a Greek olive from off of her salad, and threw it playfully at Andrew.

"You better behave or the manager is going to kick you out," Andrew said, picking up the olive and throwing it back at Alexis.

ॐ

Alexis arrived at her mother's house at 6:45 Saturday night. Lela was a bundle of nerves.

"I don't know if this is such a good idea, Alex." Lela's brow furrowed unconsciously.

"Aunt Lela, of course it is! Have you ever seen mother more excited or alert?" Alexis tried to disguise her annoyance.

Lela gave an anxious little cough. "No, but still, what if it conjures up bad memories too?"

Alexis shook her head. "I don't think so. Mom seemed to really have liked Nikoli. She even mentioned writing letters to him in Greece once she'd moved to America."

"Your mother said that?" Lela was nervously and unconsciously twisting her hands together.

"Yes. Imagine my mother having a first love. I think it's very exciting."

"You do?" Lela was flitting about the foyer and sitting room, fussing with throw pillows and knick-knacks.

"Aunt Lela, the house looks beautiful." The doorbell rang and Alexis made her way towards the front door, as Lela followed apprehensively.

"Nick, thank you for coming. It was kind of you." Alexis's smile was sincere.

Nick smiled back and held out a bouquet of flowers. "These are for your mother."

Trying not to act too surprised by Nick's thoughtfulness, Alexis reached out and took the bouquet from him. "My mother loves flowers." Then, realizing Nick was still standing outside, Alexis said, "Please come in."

Nick stepped into the foyer, looked around, and let out a low whistle. "Wow, this place is beautiful! Did your dad design it?"

"Of course. It's a replica of a mansion that he saw many years ago. He even had the winding staircase put in."

"Is this the house you grew up in?"

"Uh huh." Alexis's dark, shiny hair moved gracefully over her shoulders as she nodded her head.

"Lucky girl." Nick imagined what it must have been like to grow up in such privileged surroundings. His own upbringing had been quite different.

"Oh, Nick, I'd like you to meet my Aunt Lela. Lela, this is Nick Agorinos." Alexis stepped aside as she made the introductions.

Lela held out her hand to Nick. To her surprise, Nick tenderly took her hand and brought it up to his lips, kissing the back of it.

Lela blushed. "It's a pleasure to meet you, Mr. Agorinos."

"Please, call me Nick."

Blushing anew, Lela said, "What can I get for you to drink? I've got Greek wine chilling, and there's pop, tea, or coffee."

"I'll take a glass of wine, thanks."

Lela went off in the direction of the kitchen, leaving Nick and Alexis alone in the foyer.

"I see you're having an effect on all of the women in my family." Alexis took in his classically handsome features and generous mouth.

"Does that include you?" Nick's dark eyes locked with her sparkling green ones.

Before Alexis had time to respond, the doorbell rang and Andrew let himself in, just in time to sense the mounting tension between his sister and Nick.

"Am I interrupting something?" Andrew's eyes darted back and forth between Alexis and Nick.

"No, of course not. I'm Nick Agorinos." Nick said.

"Nick, I'm Andrew. Pleasure to meet you." Andrew and Nick shook hands.

"Hey, thanks a lot for coming out to see my mom."

"It's no big deal."

"From what Alex tells me, it is. She said she never saw my mom so excited before. I've never seen my mom enthusiastic about anything so I had to come by."

Lela returned from the kitchen with a silver serving tray. On it were five glasses of white Greek wine. "I brought each of us a glass of wine. Even one for your mother."

Andrew went over to Lela and kissed her on the cheek. "Let me help you with that," he said, taking the tray from his aunt.

"Thank you, dear." Looking at each of them in turn, Lela asked uncertainly, "Shall we get started?" Then, without waiting for an answer, she led the way into the sitting room where Diana was waiting.

Diana had chosen a simple, white cotton dress to wear. Over it, she wore a white cardigan with gold buttons. Her dark gray hair was pulled up attractively and held in place with a decorative comb. She was sitting quietly in a chair with her hands folded in front of her.

When Nick entered the room, Diana jumped excitedly from her chair. "Nikoli, you came!"

"Yes, I said I would. I brought you some flowers." Alexis came forward with the bouquet and handed them to her mother.

"Oh, they're beautiful! They're so beautiful." She cradled them in her arms and brought them up to her face, burying her nose in them.

"Why don't we all have a seat. Lela has poured us all a glass of wine."

Diana went back to her chair as Alexis and Lela sat down on the sofa. Nick sat down in the chair next to Diana, which had a small, round glass cocktail table between them.

Andrew went around the room and served the wine, then putting the tray down on the large glass coffee table, he too sat down on the sofa with Lela and Alexis.

Diana had suddenly grown somber. "Nikoli, why didn't you write to me?"

"I'm Nick, remember?" Nick said patiently.

"I wrote several letters to you, but you never wrote back. I waited as long as I could for you to come to America and be with me."

"My father was killed in the war, Diana. I'm sorry you didn't know that."

"Who was your father?"

"Nikoli, the man you knew. I never had a chance to know him myself. What was he like?"

"Who?"

"Nikoli, what was he like?" Nick was used to having to be patient with his mother. He didn't appear to be bothered at having to repeat himself.

A serene smile spread across Diana's face. "He was so handsome. You look just like him. He had dark eyes and dark hair. The first time I set eyes on him I fell in love with him. He was cleaning and repairing the nets after a night of fishing on his father's boat."

"Yes, that was my grandfather, Jason. He was a wonderful man."

"Well, when I was growing up it wasn't acceptable for a young girl and boy to have a relationship without their parent's consent. Nikoli and I had to meet in private, usually by the sea. We would read poetry to each other and talk about life and love." Diana sighed wistfully.

"My father liked poetry?" Nick absorbed this small bit of information as though it was a nugget of gold.

"Oh yes. He wrote his own poems and shared them with me."

Nick's eyes had a faraway look in them, as though he was trying to picture his father writing a poem. Over the years, he had formed a picture in his mind of who Nikoli was, molding and shaping him according to what others told him about the man he never met.

"Of course, my parents were furious when I admitted to them that I had been going down by the sea to visit Nikoli. They booked passage for me on the next ship leaving for America."

Lela interjected, "That was because of the war, Diana. They feared for your safety."

"Yes, and rightfully so. The Germans killed my parents and they probably would have killed me too." Diana's voice trembled.

"That would have been a great tragedy," Nick said, suddenly noticing the intense green color of Diana's eyes. "Alexis wouldn't have been able to inherit your beautiful green eyes."

Diana's eyes had filled with tears that glistened and magnified their color, making them look like sparkling emeralds as she looked over at Nick. "Life certainly has a way of twisting ones dreams around."

"It certainly does!" Nick agreed heartily, and held his glass to Diana's. "A toast, to old friends and reunions."

"To old friends." Diana mimicked and took a sip of her wine.

Andrew, Alexis, and Lela joined in the toast. The three had been quietly sitting and observing Diana and Nick, mesmerized by the scene that had unfolded before them.

Andrew was especially delighted to see his mother acting so coherent. A twinge of jealousy shot through him that Nick had been able to draw his mother out of her shell.

"So, what brought you to America Nick?"

"Well, I was just a kid when World War II ended. The war had been especially hard on the elderly. Many of them suffered from malnutrition and disease. Jason, my grandfather, died six years after the Germans left Greece. I was nine years old at the time of his death. My grandmother, Catherine, died one year later. After that, mom and I decided to pack up our belongings and start a new life in America."

Alexis and Andrew had the same thought simultaneously; compared to Nick's upbringing, they had lived a fortunate life. They had never had to deal with the inconvenience and uncertainties of packing up and starting over.

"That must have been difficult for you." Alexis said, wondering what it must have been like to leave your homeland and set off for the unknown.

"At my age, it was the most exciting thing in the world. I'd heard many stories about America being the land of opportunity. Mom and I had friends here who sponsored us and helped my mother find work and enrolled me into school. After I graduated from high school with honors, I earned a scholarship to a local college where I earned an architectural engineering degree."

Andrew let out a long whistle. "I'm impressed. It took a lot of guts and hard work for you to get where you are today. You're good at what you do."

"Thanks," Nick smiled, accepting the compliment.

"Alexis is working on a new mall project. Dad left us some land and she's developing it." Andrew felt Alexis shift uneasily beside him. He was bringing up a touchy subject, but he had a purpose.

"Yes, I know." Nick moved uncomfortably in his chair. He and Alexis hadn't spoken about the project since he had called to apologize to her.

"My sister is one of the most outstanding businesswomen I know. Once she makes up her mind to do something, she sticks to it with stubborn determination."

As much as Andrew admired Nick for his hard work, the fact remained that he had been rude to his sister at their first meeting.

"Does she? How is it that you ended up running the restaurant business and Alexis the building company?" Nick's perception was sharp. He was up for the mental sparring that was obviously taking place.

"Default. I was a natural at the food industry and Alexis was drawn to new construction and land development."

"I would think that it would have been the other way around. The building industry is predominantly male. Without your father to oversee future projects, Alexis is going to have to struggle to make a name for herself."

"My work speaks for itself, Nick. Anyone who's dealt with my father in the past has indirectly dealt with me as well." Alexis said, coming to her own defense.

Surprisingly, Diana had been following the conversation. Directing her comment to Nick, she said, "Your father thought I could do anything. He liked the fact that I was strong-headed and opinionated."

Nick turned his attention to her. "My mother was the opposite of that. She was quiet and somewhat fearful of life."

"Maybe that's why he never wrote to me. I probably scared him away."

"My father was very attached to his parents. I don't believe he would have just followed his whims and left them to come to America."

Diana agreed. "Probably not. He felt it was his duty to take over his father's fishing business."

"Yes, he did from what I was told. Like I said, I never got to know him." Nick swirled the remainder of the wine in his glass before finishing it.

"Where do you and your mother live?" Diana asked.

"She lives in an apartment with her cousin who looks after her. I have my own home about fifteen minutes from her place." Nick looked at his watch and stood up. "I'd better be going, I have a prior engagement."

"Oh, of course." Diana stood up. "Thank you for coming to visit me."

"It was my pleasure. I can see why my father liked you." He said graciously.

Andrew and Alexis walked Nick to the door.

"Thanks again. It was an interesting evening." Andrew said as he shook Nick's hand.

"You're welcome." Nick turned to look at Alexis. "Have you had your meeting with Daniel Blake yet?"

"No, I…actually, I never made the appointment with him."

"What are you waiting for?"

"I, uh…" Andrew looked at his sister in surprise. He had never seen Alexis at a loss for words. "Nick, the truth is that I really want to work on the new mall with *you*, but I want you to trust me."

"When were you going to call me and tell me all of this?"

Alexis was caught off guard by the sudden vibrancy of his voice. "Hey, I got sidetracked by my mother's situation. This has been a traumatic week for me."

"I'll call you on Monday and we'll set up a meeting for some time next week. I'd be honored to work on the project with you."

"You would?" she asked, surprised by this unpredictable man.

Nick's dark eyes blazed into hers, and he smiled. "Yes, I would."

Andrew hadn't missed the tension that had built between Nick and his sister as they stood staring at each other. "Ahem. I thought you had a prior engagement. You wouldn't want to be late, would you?" Andrew directed this question at Nick.

Nick pulled his gaze from Alexis. "Right, I have to get going. Good night."

After letting Nick out, Andrew shut the door and turned to face Alexis. "What in the world got into you just now? You were acting like a complete idiot!"

"What are you talking about?"

Andrew mimicked his sister. "'I, uh…no, I…'" then he fluttered his eyelashes and giggled.

Alexis punched him playfully on the arm. "I didn't do that! Please tell me I didn't look like that?"

Andrew gave her a chastising look. "Sorry, but you did. The way to win a guy like Nick over is to stay cool."

"I'm not trying to *win* him over. I want him to work with me based upon my business merits."

"I think he might be interested in your *other* merits." Andrew said, teasingly.

Alexis blushed and shook her head. Together, they walked back into the sitting room where Diana and Lela were engaged in conversation.

"Well, what did you think of Nick?" Alexis asked Lela.

"He's very nice. I think everything went well, and I'm glad you invited him over after all. Your mother enjoyed his visit."

Diana smiled up at Alexis. "Thank you for arranging tonight, dear. I'm lucky to have a daughter like you."

Tears of happiness welled up in Alexis's eyes. If only for the moment, her mother was back.

CHAPTER TWENTY-ONE

Alexis picked up her phone on the second ring. "Stephanos develop-ment company, Alex speaking."

"Alex, this is Nick."

"Nick, good to hear from you." And she meant it. "I suppose you're calling to set up that meeting?"

"Yes, I was thinking of Wednesday afternoon, say around two o'clock?"

Alexis quickly glanced at her calendar before replying. "That would be great, I'll put you in my schedule."

"Great. So, how's your mom?"

"I can't tell you what a difference your visit made. She still has her usual moments when her memory lapses, but she's been more alert than usual." Alexis replied.

"When are you taking her to see Doctor Williams again?" Nick asked.

"Next Friday." Alexis replied, and double-checked to make sure she'd written it down in her appointment book.

"I can come by on Saturday night again to visit her if you'd like."

"Are you sure? I'd hate to think of you giving up two Saturday nights in a row like that." What Alexis really wanted to ask Nick was whether or not he had a girlfriend and if so, why wasn't he spending his Saturday nights with her.

"Alex, I wouldn't have offered if it was going to be a problem. Okay?"

"Okay. Thanks Nick, I'll see you on Wednesday at our meeting. We can talk more about it then." Alexis was preparing to end the conversation.

"Alex, wait, don't hang up yet. I was wondering if you'd like to have dinner with me before Wednesday." There was a hint of foreign anxiety in Nick's voice.

"You mean as in dinner for the sake of eating, or would it be business?"

"I mean dinner as in pleasure. My place, I'll cook."

Alexis was totally taken aback by his offer. "I don't know what to say. I've never had a guy cook for me before besides my dad and my brother."

"Well, this will be a first for both of us then. I've never cooked for a woman before." Nick's nervous laugh betrayed him.

"Sounds dangerous." Alexis liked this vulnerable side of Nick.

"It could be, but it'll be fun too, how about it?"

"Okay, what time do you want me there?"

"Is 6:00 Tuesday night okay?"

Again, Alexis referred to her schedule. "Sure, that'd be fine. How do I get to your house?"

Nick gave Alexis directions to an upscale neighborhood fifteen minutes from her own home. "Call me if you run into any problems."

"I will. See you tomorrow." Hanging up the phone, Alexis nervously bit her lower lip. So far, everything was going smoothly with Nick. He seemed open to helping her with the mall project, had come over to visit her mother, and now he was offering to make dinner for her. She wondered if there was a catch in all of this good fortune. Deciding to take it all at face value, Alexis picked up the phone to call her brother.

On Tuesday evening, Alexis found herself in front of Nick's house situated in a neighborhood very similar to her own. Although hers was a spacious two-story home, Nick's house was a sprawling ranch situated on a large lot surrounded by plenty of trees.

Built of dark brown brick and wood trim stained dark brown to match, the house was strong and masculine looking.

Brass light fixtures lit the porch on either side of the front entryway. The tall oak front door had a heavy brass knocker and brass door handle. Alexis rang the doorbell which chimed loudly to announce her arrival.

Alexis was greeted warmly by Nick. "Come on in. I hope you didn't have any trouble finding the place."

"Nope, you give great directions." She smiled and took off her coat, handing it to Nick who hung it up in the foyer closet. A small decorative mirror was affixed to the wall in the foyer with a small antique table situated beneath it. Alexis ran her finger along it admirably.

"My father made that. It was one of the few pieces of furniture we were allowed to bring over." Nick explained.

"It's beautiful." An awkward silence loomed between them as they stood staring wordlessly at each other. "Something smells good."

"Oh my gosh, I almost forgot about the dinner rolls!" Nick made a dash for the kitchen with Alexis following closely behind him.

Nick grabbed an oven mitt and pulled the pan out of the oven. He loosened one of the rolls to check the bottom of it and held it up for Alexis to inspect.

"Looks like you got here just in time. They're still edible." Alexis took the dinner roll and spread butter on it. Then tearing it in half, she gave a piece to Nick and bit into the hot bread. "Mmm, what else are we going to have?"

Nick had been watching Alexis, admiring the sensuous way she'd eaten the bread.

Alexis snapped her fingers in front of his face. "Hello, anybody home?"

"I was lost in thought there for a second, sorry." He searched for a plausible explanation and when he realized he didn't have one, he said, "We're having Delmonico steak cooked to perfection. It's been marinating in white wine and herbs all day. I've also prepared green beans with slivered almonds cooked in olive oil, and there's fresh salad."

Alexis cocked her head in approval. "Need help with the final touches?"

Glad for the diversion, Nick said, "Sure, how about putting the salad and green beans on the table. I'll put the rolls in a bread basket and take the steak out of the broiler."

Alexis and Nick went about their tasks and when they were done, they sat down at the beautifully set table complete with white linen tablecloth and napkins. Nick had even lit two tapered candles placed into crystal candleholders giving the room a soft glow.

"You don't get out very much do you?" Alexis said as she took another bite of her food.

"Why do you say that?"

"Because I've caught you staring at me three times already."

Nick looked away, embarrassed. "You're right. I'm sorry but I find myself at a loss for words around you."

"Well don't be. I don't want to have to bear the burden of the entire conversation for the whole evening."

Not wanting Alexis to feel uncomfortable, Nick decided to tread on ground that was common to both of them. "So, tell me about some of the other projects you've worked on."

"Well, most of them were small strip malls or office buildings. My dad spent his entire life working to build his restaurant business and buying up undeveloped property with the profits."

"He was a smart man. What a great legacy to leave to his children."

Alexis felt the lump rise in her throat and she had to put down her fork. Unexpected tears had welled up in her eyes.

Nick sat awkwardly across from her not knowing what to say or do. "I'm sorry, did I say something wrong?"

"No, of course not." Alexis shook her head adamantly. "You couldn't possibly have known how close I was with my father and how much I miss him. You didn't say anything wrong. He was a smart man and I appreciate everything he's left me and my brother."

You had the momentum of a prior generation to push you forward. In many ways, I'm envious of you."

Alexis smirked. "That's a far cry from the man who was in my office last week."

"You mean the one who didn't want to deal with a woman in business?" Nick's tone was playful.

"Yeah, that one. It seems like he's changed his mind."

"More like a change of heart." Nick's eyes filled with a sudden intense sparkling.

"Why, Nick? I've been suspicious of your motives ever since you called me to apologize." Alexis refused to be taken in by this man who seemed impossible to get to know intimately. She'd only met him one week ago and already he'd shown a mercurial temperament.

"I don't know. There's something about you that I can't resist. I've never called a woman to apologize for my behavior in the past because I didn't care if I'd hurt them. For some unknown reason, I care about whether or not I hurt you."

"I need to know why, Nick. What's changed?" She asked, wanting to put all of the pieces together.

"I can't explain it, Alexis." He was running out of diversions. "Besides, how do you explain the fact that we ran into each other at the doctor's office and that our mother's grew up in the same village, and my father and your mother were once very deeply in love?" Nick realized he'd said too much and looked away. He hadn't meant for it to happen like this.

"What's that supposed to mean?"

Nick shook his head then returned his gaze to Alexis. "I have something to show you." Getting up from the table, he motioned for Alexis to follow him to his bedroom.

"If this is some idiotic way of trying to get me into bed, you'll be sorry!"

Nick didn't reply as he continued walking down the thickly carpeted hallway. Once in his bedroom, he pulled out his desk chair for Alexis to sit down. Then, going over to his closet, he pulled out a large steamer trunk and opened the lid. From inside, he lifted out a small wooden box and a packet of letters and went over to stand by Alexis.

Curiously, Alexis watched as Nick set the items down on the desk next to where she was sitting.

"Do you know what these are?" Nick asked Alexis.

"They look like letters to me." Alexis still wasn't comprehending what Nick was up to.

"Look at them, Alexis. I've been carrying them around since I moved here from Greece. My mother was obsessed with the relationship between your mother and my father. She hid these letters from my dad so that he wouldn't come to America looking for her!"

Slowly, realization set in and Alexis picked up one of the letters with a shaking hand. The familiar handwriting was that of her mother's. Although the paper was yellow with age, the writing was still legible. With trembling hands, she removed the letter from its envelope.

My dearest Nikoli,

I hope that by now you are back from the war. To me the war is a dark and ugly monster that separated me from the one I love, and I hate it! I am now on a train headed for Chicago, where my Aunt Lela lives. My parents intend for me to marry a café owner there, but I will not do it. How can I when it is you that I love?

I think about you nearly every waking hour. Oh, Nikoli, come to me as soon as you get this letter. You must save me, save my life! Please, please come to me as soon as possible. I love you, and always will.

Forever yours,
Diana

Placing the letter back into its envelope, Alexis picked up another and read it. One after another, she read until she was consumed with an undeniable anger. Each letter was filled with proclamations of Diana's love for Nikoli, and each letter begged him to return her correspondence, or for him to come to America and rescue her.

Looking at the box, and then at Nick, she asked in a tremulous voice, "What's in there?"

Nick shrugged, "I believe they're keepsakes that belonged to my father. There's no explanation for them. My mother found it behind a loose stone in the wall of the bedroom she shared with my father."

Alexis removed the lid and peered inside. Picking up the rock she held it in the palm of her hand and studied it. There were no words etched on it to indicate what it had meant to its owner. There was a feather and the remainder of what looked to have once been a purple flower, now mostly dust at the bottom of the box. There was also a piece of parchment rolled up and secured with a red ribbon. Gently, Alexis removed the ribbon and unrolled the parchment.

Diana's Love

Your love is as gentle as an early summer breeze,
as exhilarating as the waves that crash against the rocks,
and as comforting as the knowledge that the sun will rise in the east
and set in the west.

Your love consumes me.

Alexis's face became an effigy of contempt. "I wish you hadn't shown this to me, Nick."

"I meant to wait until we'd had a chance to get to know each other better before sharing it with you, but I felt that I'd said too much at the dinner table and had to explain myself." He admitted the truth hopefully.

"All this," Alexis waved her hand over the letters and the box of keepsakes, "makes me feel angry and hurt. Angry with your mother for hiding these letters from your father and hurt that my mother loved him so much. I want to believe that my mother loved *my* father this much."

"They were young, Alexis. You can't take this so seriously."

"Your mother did! She took it seriously enough to hide the truth from your father so that he wouldn't know how my mother really felt about him."

"Things were different back then. A young girl and boy were not allowed to choose whom they were going to marry, it was decided for them. No matter how your mother felt about my father and vise versa, they probably would never have been allowed to marry each other. And more than likely, they wouldn't have gone against their parents wishes."

Alexis shook her head. "It all seems so deceitful." Then standing up, she said, "I'd like to go home now. Thanks for the meal."

"But we haven't finished eating it yet!" Nick said in protest.

"I couldn't eat another bite if my life depended on it. Good night, Nick." Alexis made her way down the hallway towards the front door. Nick followed anxiously.

"Alexis, please don't go. Let's talk about this. I don't think it's a good idea for you to just leave."

Alexis wasn't listening. She had her own opinion of the situation and she wasn't going to be swayed. Picking up her purse from the kitchen counter, she let herself out the front door.

Nick stood there speechless, watching her. Then remembering that she'd left without her coat he quickly went to retrieve it from the foyer closet. Running out the front door and onto the front walkway, he held up the coat as Alexis was driving away.

She didn't even glance back as Nick made his way dejectedly back into the house.

CHAPTER TWENTY-TWO

Nick had decided not to call Alexis the next morning in order to give her time to cool off, think things over. Instead, he had a large basket of flowers sent to her office. It wasn't *his* fault that his mother had been so deceptive. Besides, it had all happened so long ago.

Since he hadn't heard from her, Nick assumed his meeting with Alexis was still on, and went to her office at 2:00 that afternoon.

"Oh, Mr. Agorinos. I left a message with your secretary about today's meeting." Beth, Alexis's secretary, informed Nick.

"I haven't been to my office today. I had some prints I needed to go over without interruption so I worked at home." Nick explained.

"Miss Stephanos had to go out of town unexpectedly."

"Out of town, to where?"

"She…I'm sorry, but that's not for me to disclose." Beth said apologetically. She liked Nick, but orders were orders, and she'd been told not to let anyone know where Alexis had gone. Especially, and most specifically, not Nick Agorinos.

"I understand. If she calls, please let her know I was here." There was an almost imperceptible note of pleading in his voice.

"I will. By the way, the flowers are beautiful." Beth smiled at Nick as he left the office.

Damn her! Nick thought as he drove. Well, there was more than one person who knew where Alexis was. He suddenly felt hungry and a visit to the Café Skyros seemed like the place to go. Hopefully, Andrew would be at the location on this side of town.

Pulling into the parking lot of the restaurant, Nick felt a wave of anxiety. What was he doing? It wasn't like him to chase after a woman like this. Alexis was different. She wasn't just any woman. She was smart, caring, and to top it off, beautiful. With a renewed sense of purpose, he strode up to the front door.

Andrew was reviewing some paperwork in one of the booths while eating a sandwich and looked up when Nick came in. He stood up and walked towards him,

"Nick, come and have a seat with me."

Nick followed Andrew back to the booth he'd been sitting in. A waitress came up to their table and offered Nick something to drink.

"I'll have a glass of iced tea, thank you." Nick waited for the waitress to leave before he started talking. "Andrew, please tell me where your sister is."

Andrew looked down at his sandwich and picked at a piece of lettuce. "First tell me what you did or said to piss her off so much."

Nick ran his hand down his face in a gesture of aggravation. "And risk having you both hate my guts? Can't you just tell me where she is and I'll go to her and patch things up."

"This isn't a business deal. We're talking about my sister. If you want to know where she is, you first have to tell me what happened. Alex doesn't get upset over minor things, she's a strong person." Andrew was talking through gritted teeth, his voice was low and angry.

The waitress set the glass of iced tea in front of Nick who smiled his thanks to her. After putting a packet of sugar in the glass and stirring it with the straw, he said,

"It's a long story."

"I've got all day." Andrew said, leaning slightly forward indicating that he was ready to listen.

Nick paused to gather his thoughts before he started talking. He hoped that Andrew's reaction would be different from his sister's.

"When my mom first started showing signs of illness over a year ago, I went through her personal belongings. I also wanted to know about some of the stuff I had in my steamer trunk. My mother liked to save things, and I wanted her to explain what certain items meant to her before she was mentally incapable of doing so."

"What kinds of things?" Andrew asked.

"You know, letters, poems, books."

Andrew nodded, his eyes never leaving Nick's face, looking for signs of dishonesty.

Nick continued. "When we left Greece, we were only allowed to bring over so many items. Since I was so young, I didn't have as much to pack and mom put some of her things in my trunk. There were some letters that I had never paid much attention to and a small box of keepsakes. When I asked my mother about them, she said that the letters were from a woman named Diana who used to be in love with my father. The box of keepsakes she was unsure of, but she thought that the items inside were things that reminded my father of Diana."

"I'm not quite sure I'm following you. We've already established that my mom and your dad liked each other quite a bit. What does any of this have to do with Alexis?"

"I showed the letters and keepsakes to Alexis last night. I invited her over to my house for dinner. She read the letters your mom wrote to my dad, and then she also read a poem that was written by my dad, which he must have intended to give to your mom. It's apparent that Diana and Nikoli were very deeply in love."

"Why didn't your dad come to find my mother then? Was it like my mother said, she was too strong-headed and he got scared away?"

Nick shook his head. "My father never saw a single one of those letters."

"Why not?"

"Because, my mother intercepted them. She was living with my grandparents at the time and had fallen in love with my father.

Whenever my grandmother asked her to go pick up the mail from the post office, and there was a letter from Diana, my mother hid it."

"Didn't your father question the lack of correspondence? I mean, if they loved each other so much I'd think that your dad would have expected my mother to write to him."

Nick shrugged, "I don't know. Things were different then. You did what your parents told you to do. Marriages were arranged and it was just too damn bad if you didn't like the person your parents chose."

Andrew drew in a deep breath. "So, maybe my mom's parents had other plans for her and sent her to America to marry my dad."

"Probably. You could ask your mom or your aunt about that."

"Look, Alexis probably got over-emotional when she read the letters and realized that your mother had been extremely deceptive. She also probably hated seeing in black and white how much my mom loved your dad. Alexis was very close with my dad and would defend him no matter what."

"I understand. Alexis feels like your mother betrayed him."

"Exactly." Andrew took another bite out of his sandwich.

"In some ways, I felt betrayed also. Maybe my dad wouldn't have been killed in the war if he'd gone to America in search of your mother." Nick smiled tentatively.

"Yeah, maybe." Andrew said, his voice far away. "I guess this whole thing is kinda weird when you really think about it."

"Yes, it is. Things could have been different for all of us. I could possibly have been born in America and had the opportunity that you and your sister had instead of having to struggle the way I did." His voice held a faint note of contempt.

"Are you angry with your mother for what she did?"

"A little. She always seemed so timid and shy, but she really had this devious side to her. When the first letter from Diana arrived, my grandmother told my mother to burn it. Instead, she hid it in the pocket of her skirt and read it later. She could have shown it to my dad."

"Your mom saw an opportunity to marry the man she was in love with and she took it. The fact that she kept the letters all these years indicates that she may have wanted them to be found eventually."

"I think so too." Nick took a long sip of his iced tea. "Speaking of being found, that leads us back to your sister. Are you going to tell me where she is?"

Andrew looked at Nick speculatively before answering. "She left for Greece this morning."

"What?" Alexis never ceased to amaze him. Nick couldn't believe she'd just take off and leave the country like that.

Andrew chuckled at Nick's reaction. "Yup. She booked a flight first thing this morning, packed a couple of suitcases, grabbed her passport, and left. Of course, she called me and my aunt Lela to say good-bye. Needless to say we were shocked at her sudden decision to leave and demanded an explanation. Especially with my mom not doing so well lately."

"And what kind of an explanation did she give you?"

"I don't think you want to know," a smirk crossed Andrew's face as he spoke.

"Actually, I do." Nick insisted.

"She said, and I quote, 'All I have to say is Nick Agorinos is the biggest jerk on earth and I never want to see him or talk to him again.'" Andrew held up his hands in mock defense, "I was just telling you what she said."

Nick's shoulders slumped in defeat. "She hates my guts. I happened to have really taken a liking to your sister."

"That was obvious." Andrew said sarcastically.

Nick stood up. "I better get going. If Alexis calls you, please tell her that we spoke and maybe put in a good word for me, would you?" he added hopefully.

"Sure. You know, I didn't like you at first because of what Alex told me about your first meeting with her and how you said that you didn't work with women. I happen to have a lot of faith in my sister and any-one who treats her poorly goes directly on my shit list."

"I deserved to be, but I called to apologize to her, and I even made dinner for her. I'm not very good with women. I always say or do the wrong thing."

"I know what you mean." Andrew agreed sympathetically. "I'll let Alexis know that we spoke. I'm sure she'll call when she arrives in Greece."

"Thanks," Nick said, then strode purposefully out to his car.

CHAPTER TWENTY-THREE

Nick drove in circles for nearly twenty minutes, trying to gather his thoughts. At first, he was going to go to his office and pick up his messages. Then, he was going to go and visit Alexis's mom and take the letters to her. Finally, he decided that he had to find out exactly where Diana was in Greece, because he was going to go after her. He couldn't let another day go by without seeing her, giving her more time to form her own twisted opinion of the situation. Never had anyone affected him as much as Alexis had.

Hopefully, his mother and his cousin would understand that he had to leave town suddenly. Nick decided that he'd better see them first before he arranged his travel plans. With that decision made, he headed towards their apartment.

His cousin, Tina, greeted Nick at the door. "Your mom's watching television in her bedroom. Can I get you something to drink?"

"No thanks. I'm not going to stay very long. Listen, I have to go out of town for a week or so. Would it be a problem if I didn't stop by? I'll deposit money into your checking account before I leave so you'll have enough for my mom and yourself."

"It wouldn't be a problem at all. Your mother will be just fine. She's really very quiet and pleasant. You go and do what you have to do." Nick's cousin was a woman in her fifties. She had never married and thrived on taking care of others, which was extremely helpful to Nick. In return, he made sure that Tina never had to worry about finances.

"Thanks, Tina," Nick said, then went off to find Sophia in her bedroom.

Sophia was sitting quietly watching an afternoon talk show. Every now and then she would mumble something to herself.

"Hi, mom." Nick went over to his mother and gave her a kiss on the cheek.

Sophia pulled away defensively to look at Nick. Then recognizing him, she relaxed. "Nick, I was wondering when you were going to come and see me. It's been so long."

"Mom, I was just here two nights ago. Don't you remember?" Nick was used to this kind of thing with his mother. He was very patient with her.

"No I don't. I think you're just saying that so I won't be upset with you."

Seeing the flowers he had bought for her, Nick pointed them out to Sophia. "Remember, I brought you those flowers when I came over."

"You did? Well, that was very nice of you." Sophia seemed to soften a bit more.

"So, how are you?"

"I'm okay." Nick paused, making sure he was doing the right thing. This whole thing could backfire miserably. "Mom, I had dinner with Alexis last night and I showed her the letters from Diana."

"Who?"

"Alexis, Diana's daughter."

"Diana! Oh my, you showed her the letters?"

"No, I showed her daughter the letters. She got angry with me and now she's gone to Greece."

"Well, you had better go after her. Don't let her get away."

"Mom, do you mean it? I really want to go and find Alexis and talk to her, but I might be gone for a while." Nick knew that his mother would probably forget what she'd said to him, but all that mattered to him was hearing her say that it was okay for him to leave.

"It was wrong of me to hide those letters from your father. His mother wanted me to burn them! He and Diana would never have been allowed to marry each other. Oh, how I wished that your father loved me as much as he loved Diana. He was so heartbroken when he found out that she'd gone to America." Tears had formed in Sophia's eyes.

"I love you mom," Nick knelt beside her frail body and held her close to him for a long time. He knew then that his mother hadn't hidden the letters to be malicious. She thought she was doing the right thing, and yet her poetic nature could not deny the fact that Nikoli and Diana loved each other. If she had obeyed Catherine, the letters would have been burned and there would have been no trace of them at all. Yet, if she had shown them to Nikoli, he wouldn't have gone against his parent's wishes by leaving Greece to be with Diana in America.

"Your father was killed before I ever had a chance to explain things to him. I meant to show him the letters when he returned home from the war, but he never came back." Sophia's voice caught in a sob.

Nick continued to hold her and stroke his mother's back. "It's okay," he whispered to her. It had been months since his mother had displayed a prolonged moment of awareness. Moments like this reminded him of who his mother had once been and it saddened him to know she would never be the same again.

"You go and find that girl and tell her that you want her to give you a chance. She'll be impressed enough by the fact that you went chasing her halfway 'round the world." Sophia dabbed at the tears that had been coursing down her cheeks.

"I hope so, mom. I haven't been back to Greece since we left."

"It's beautiful there, but I'm not sorry we left. I don't exactly have fond memories it."

"I know, mom. I know." Nick was still kneeling beside his mother. He took her hand in his and said, "I was upset with you at first when I found out about the letters. I felt it was wrong of you to do something so deceptive."

"Times were different back then. Your grandmother Catherine was a very strong woman and determined to have her way. She didn't like Diana because she thought she was wild. In a way, for those days, she was a bit wild."

"How do you mean?" Nick was determined to soak up as much information as he could while his mother was still aware of what she was saying.

"Well, Diana was very pretty, outgoing, and smart. She worked in her father's café and knew a lot of people. Diana wasn't afraid of anything or anyone and tended to follow her heart. Unfortunately, that kind of behavior was frowned upon by older people because it didn't fit in with their plans."

"You mean plans to have children and work hard?"

Sophia laughed softly, then said, "Yes, that's about it."

"I'm glad you're my mom. Thank you."

"You're a good son, Nick." Something across the room had caught Sophia's attention. "Oh, would you look at that. I must have forgotten to water that plant over there!"

Nick knew the moment was over. His mother was lost again in her own private world, a place he couldn't follow her to. "I'll tell Tina about the plant."

Sophia looked at Nick, confused. "What plant?"

"I have to go now, mom. I'll see you when I get back." He gave her another quick peck on the cheek.

"Get back from where?"

Nick was already on his way down the hallway. Tina walked him to the door.

"I'll be in touch with you once I know where I'm staying in Greece. I'll be back in about a week."

"Don't you worry about a thing. Okay?" Tina smiled and gave him a hug good-bye.

After leaving his mother, Nick stopped by his office to inform his secretary that he had to go out of town. From there, he returned home to pack a couple of suitcases and make sure his passport was still current. He had to find Andrew so that he could find out where Alexis was staying and book his flight.

But first, he had to go and see Diana. With the letters and box of keepsakes, he sped through the streets of Chicago.

Lela answered the door, and when she saw Nick standing at the door, reluctantly let him inside the house.

"I spoke with Andrew this afternoon and he told me that Alexis left for Greece."

"She's upset with you, but she didn't say why." Lela said.

"We had a misunderstanding at my house last night." Nick started to explain.

"What kind of misunderstanding?" Lela placed a hand on her hip.

"I showed her these." Nick held up the packet of letters and box of mementos.

Lela's hand slid from her hip down to her side, and her eyebrows drew together inquisitively as she moved towards Nick.

"I need to see Diana." Nick said, pulling the items protectively towards his chest.

Awareness broke over Lela's face when she realized the handwriting on the top envelope was Diana's. "If those are what I think they are, then I think you'd better leave right now. You'll cause nothing but trouble, Nick." Lela's words were as cool and clear as ice.

The doorbell rang startling them both, then Andrew let himself in. "Aunt Lela," then noticing she wasn't alone, "Nick, what are you doing here?"

"I came to show your mother the letters and this box of memories. I thought it was time that she knew the truth. Maybe it will help her to sort things out in her mind."

"I think that's a great idea," Andrew said encouragingly.

"Well I don't!" Lela stamped her foot.

"Aunt Lela, why in the world would it matter to you if my mother saw those letters?" Andrew asked, surprised at his aunt's reaction.

"I don't owe you or anybody else an explanation. I just don't think it's a good idea. It might upset her."

Andrew and Nick exchanged a contemplative look.

"Aunt Lela, do you know something about this whole situation that you'd like to share with us?" Andrew asked, his voice maintained a conciliatory tone.

In response, Lela turned her back on the two men. "I'm not saying another word. Show her the letters if you must, but don't be surprised if she gets upset and becomes inconsolable."

Nick and Andrew went to the sitting room where Diana spent most of her time.

As usual, she was seated in her favorite chair working on needlepoint.

"Hi, mom." Andrew bent to kiss his mother on the cheek.

Diana looked up, "Andrew, what a nice surprise. I'm making a decorative pillow cover for my bed. What do you think?" She held up her work for him to inspect.

"It's beautiful, you're really talented." Andrew complimented her. Diana hadn't even been aware of Nick. "Mom, look who else is here."

Nick came forward to say hello. "Good to see you again, Diana."

Diana let her needlepoint drop to her lap. "Nikoli!"

"I'm Nick, remember?"

Diana blushed, "Of course I remember you."

"I have something to show you." Nick came closer to where Diana was sitting. He held out the box of memories first. "Does this look familiar to you?"

Diana took the box from him and ran her hand over it. She shook her head, "I don't think I've ever seen it before."

Nick removed the lid while leaving the rest of the box in her hand. She placed the box with its contents on her lap on top of her needlepoint. With a shaking hand, she removed the rock. It was shiny green, and she smoothed her thumb over its glassy surface. "I found this rock on the beach one day and gave it to Nikoli in memory of our time spent near the sea. He said that the green shade reminded him of the color of my eyes." She held the rock up for Nick and Andrew to look at.

Picking up the long white feather, she said, "This was just a bird's feather that was lying on the beach, and I had playfully run it across Nikoli's cheek. He grabbed it out of my hand and placed it in his pocket." Diana smiled and ran it across her own, closing her eyes in fond memory.

Placing the feather back in the box, she picked up what remained of the purple flower. Diana held it up to her now gray hair. "I used to wear purple flowers in my hair quite often. One night, before returning to my parent's home, I removed the flower from my hair and gave it to Nikoli. I can't believe he saved it!"

Andrew and Nick watched, captivated by Diana's ability to bring life to the items that were in the box. Finally, Diana picked up the parchment bound by the red ribbon.

Carefully removing the ribbon, she unrolled the paper and read the poem.

"Mom, are you okay." Andrew said, the first hint of concern lacing his voice.

Diana was frozen, her hand paused in mid-air holding the poem. "I...I never saw this before."

"Did my father write it?" Nick asked anxiously.

"Yes, it's his handwriting. I wonder when he wrote this." She turned the paper over in her hand. There was a date on the back. "It says December, 1940.

That must mean he wrote it when he returned home from the war. I thought he was killed?" Diana looked up at Nick for an answer.

"He was, but not until April of 1941. The fighting ended briefly in 1940 but started up again shortly after. My father was killed the second time he went back to fight." Nick's voice grew tight with emotion.

"If that's so, then why didn't he return any of my letters?" Diana asked, dismayed.

"Because, he never got them." Nick held out the letters to her, which she took.

"But why? I addressed them to his mother. Why wouldn't she give them to him?"

Nick shrugged, not wanting to answer the inevitable question, and looked at Andrew for help. Things were getting uncomfortable.

"Mom, Nikoli's mother didn't want him to see the letters. She wanted Nikoli to marry Sophia. She instructed Sophia to burn them, but instead she hid them."

"That still doesn't explain why Nikoli didn't try to contact me." Diana's face clouded.

Lela interjected. "Nikoli didn't bother writing to you because your mother told him you'd gone to America to seek a better life—one that didn't include him."

Nick, Andrew, and Diana all looked over at her in surprise. None of them had heard her come into the room.

"My mother told him that?" Diana choked on the words. "Why?"

A shadow of annoyance crossed Lela's face. "That's just the way it was back then, Diana. Young people weren't free to love whomever they chose. It was believed that parents knew what was best for their children."

"And my parents thought it was best for me to come to America and marry André, with your help of course." Permanent sorrow weighed Diana down as she sank back into her chair.

"How dare you complain, Diana. If your parents hadn't sent you away you'd be dead just as they are. André took wonderful care of you and your children." Lela said in as reasonable a tone as possible.

"He also took wonderful care of you too, didn't he? That was all part of the deal wasn't it?" Andrew challenged her, but he was confused. What stance should he take in all of this, if any?

Lela remained silent.

"I'd rather have died loving the man I was meant to love, living the life I was meant to live, than playing out somebody else's charade." Diana replied in a low, tormented voice.

"How can you say that in front of your own son?" Lela was appalled.

Diana drew in a sharp breath. "Andrew, I'm sorry you had to hear all of this. I'm afraid I've already said too much."

Andrew had walked over to the sitting room window, his back to the room. "All I want to know is did you love my dad at all?"

"Oh, Andrew, of course I did. He was a wonderful man. What wasn't there to love about your father."

The tension in Andrew's shoulders seemed to visibly drain as he turned to face her. "That's all that matters to me, mom."

Nick smiled, glad that Andrew was taking control of the situation. "What should I do with these." He held up the letters. The box was still on Diana's lap.

Andrew took the letters from Nick's hand and handed them to Diana. "Mother, these letters and the items in that box rightfully belong to you. I hope you can put the past to rest now that you know the truth. Nikoli did love you very much. It just wasn't meant to be. I loved and respected my father very much and I for one am not sorry that things turned out the way that they did." Andrew was still standing in front of Diana.

Diana took the letters from his hand. "I'm not sorry either, Andrew. I love you and I'm proud of you."

Purposefully, Diana rose from her chair and went over to Lela. Lela had been standing quietly, if not defensively, in the doorway of the room. "I know that you did what you thought was best for me. You kept your promise to my parents to look after me. What's done is done, I can't bring Nikoli back. If he had been a stronger man, he would have sought me out no matter what anyone had said to him."

Lela reached out to lovingly squeeze Diana's arm.

Diana then turned to face Nick. "You have a chance to change your future. If you care about Alexis, which I believe you do, you'll go after her and you won't come back without her. I'm warning you though, she's very strong-headed."

"Like her mother?" the warmth of Nick's smile was reflected in his voice.

"Yes, like her mother." Diana returned his smile.

"Where can I find her?" Nick turned to face Andrew.

"The Heraklion International Airport in Crete. From there you will go to the village of Dyonisos where Alex has rented an apartment."

CHAPTER TWENTY-FOUR

Nick looked out of the airplane window as it started its descent in preparation for landing. He hadn't been to Greece since leaving it as a child. In all actuality, it did not hold the aura of charm and beauty that it did for the many tourists who flocked there each year. Nick's memories were from the perspective of a child who had left his homeland in search of a better life in America.

Sitting back in his seat, Nick reflected on the past year which had so far been very eventful. Time Inc. had transmitted HBO, the first pay cable network. Believing that this was going to be the wave of the future, Nick had judiciously bought up several hundred shares of stock in the company. The compact disc was developed by RCA and had yet to make the mainstream. June 1972 marked the start of the Watergate scandal and President Nixon had made an unprecedented eight-day visit to communist China to meet with Mao Tse-Tung.

The captain's voice coming over the intercom broke into Nick's thoughts. "Ladies and gentlemen, at this time I'd like to ask you to fasten your seatbelts. We hope that your flight has been comfortable. The temperature at the Heraklion International Airport is a pleasant 78 degrees. Please put your chair in the upright position and remain seated as we prepare to land. Thank you."

Nick made sure his seatbelt was fastened and his chair upright. Glancing out the window for a second time, he could see the beautiful, sparkling blue water of the Mediterranean. Crete is an island of diverse beauty. Miles of white, sandy beaches welcome swimming, sailing, snorkeling, and many other water sports. The mountainous terrain beckons to those who enjoy climbing.

The southernmost Greek island is divided into four prefectures: Hania, Rethymo, Iraklio, and Lassithi. In Greek Mythology, Crete is known as the birthplace of Zeus.

The airplane made a smooth landing on the runway and eventually came to a halt at the terminal. Once Nick had collected his luggage, he stepped outside to hail a cab.

The airport was swarming with taxis and it wasn't long before he was seated and on his way to see Alexis. The village of Dyonisos is located in a nature reserve far removed from mass tourism on the east coast of Crete.

When she wants to get away, she really gets away! Nick thought to himself about Alexis as the cab drove along. She couldn't have picked a more remote spot unless it had been to one of the monasteries hidden away in the mountains.

Forty-five minutes and a hefty cab fare later, Nick found himself in front of a two-story red brick home that had been converted into an upper and lower apartment. Nick carried his suitcases to the front door of the lower apartment where Alexis was staying and rang the doorbell.

Several minutes later, Nick was nervously tapping his foot and looking at his watch. Agonizing questions that he had no answers to ran rampantly through his mind.

What if Alexis was inside and could see him and chose not to answer the door? What if she was with someone else? What had he gotten himself into?

Turning the handle of the door, Nick found that it was unlocked and let himself in. He set his two suitcases down in the foyer and called out, "Alexis? Anybody home?"

Nick's voice echoed through the empty apartment. *I guess I'll just have to wait until she gets back from wherever she's at.* Nick thought to himself.

The apartment was simply yet tastefully decorated. The floor of the foyer was covered in gray slate and led into a small kitchen, which gave way to a spacious living room. The kitchen was complete with sink, refrigerator, dishwasher, stove and oven.

Instead of a kitchen table, there was a long counter with several comfortably padded barstools along one side of it.

Plush off-white carpeting matched the cream leather sofa and loveseat in the living room. An octagonal glass and brass coffee table was set in the center of the room in front of the furniture. A sliding door offered a magnificent view of the ocean, and Nick could see someone horseback riding on the beach.

There was only one bedroom but Nick refrained from checking it out. He didn't want to be caught snooping into Alexis's personal stuff if she happened to return while he was in there. Returning to the foyer where he'd left his luggage, Nick picked up his carry on bag, which had his personal grooming gear in it, and went into the bathroom located off of the foyer.

Although she'd only been in Greece for one day, Alexis had already made herself at home in the bathroom. The cream marble counter was covered with hair styling implements, skin care products, toothbrush, and toothpaste. A wet bathing suit had been hung over the opaque shower doors to dry.

Moving some of Alexis's things aside, Nick set his own items on the counter. First, he brushed his teeth and gargled with mouthwash. Next, he washed his face and neck with the bar of soap. He ran a comb through his thick dark hair and as a final touch splashed on some cologne.

Just as he had finished putting away his things, Nick heard someone come inside the front door of the apartment.

"Is somebody here?" Alexis called out in alarm. She hadn't been expecting anyone and was surprised to see two unfamiliar suitcases in the foyer.

Nick blew out a nervous breath before answering. "Alex, it's me."

"Me who?"

"Nick." There was absolute silence as Nick opened the bathroom door and stepped out into the foyer where Alexis was still standing.

"What in the *hell* are *you* doing here?" Alexis jabbed an accusing finger into the air at Nick.

"We need to talk."

"No we don't!" Alexis was so furious she could barely speak.

"Please Alexis," Nick pleaded. "I changed my entire schedule so that I could come all the way over her to see you."

"You have one minute to use my phone to call a cab and get *out* of here!"

"Alexis, please give me a chance to…"

"*One minute!*" Alexis replied with contempt that forbade further comment.

Moving over to the phone, Nick picked it up and dialed the operator who then connected him with the local cab company.

"The cab should be here in about five minutes."

"That means ten minutes around here the way everyone takes their time." Alexis said with distaste.

"Well that's one of the reasons you chose this place, wasn't it?" Nick attempted to make light conversation with Alexis.

"No! I came here to get away. Mostly from you!" Alexis shot him a cold look.

Nick searched for something to say as he and Alexis stared at each other. Alexis's green eyes had darkened with anger.

Nick took an abrupt step towards Alexis, who moved backwards, away from him.

"I'm sorry if you were offended by the letters I showed you. I didn't think you'd get so angry about them."

"That's right, you *didn't* think. The only thing you were concerned about was that you'd found Diana. In case you haven't figured it out, I don't care one single bit about your father's feelings for my mother. The whole situation is unsettling and I want to forget about it." Alexis walked with stiff dignity into the kitchen where she poured herself a glass of juice.

"I spoke to your brother and we showed the letters to your mom."

Alexis's hand froze with the glass halfway up to her mouth. "I am personally going to strangle my brother when I get home. He never should have let you show my mother those letters and I wish he'd never told you where to find me."

A horn honked outside indicating that the cab had arrived. Nick strode to the front door and opened it. Picking up his suitcases he turned towards Alexis. "You can kick me out of your apartment but you can't kick me off of this island."

Alexis remained absolutely motionless for a moment. Then with one graceful spin of her heel, she turned her back on Nick.

CHAPTER TWENTY-FIVE

Fortunately, Nick had been able to find a room at a bed and breakfast in the village, five minutes from where Alexis was staying. Certainly, he hadn't been expecting her to welcome him with open arms, but he *had* expected her to at least hear him out.

He had spent the remainder of his first day going to the local museum and then having a large dinner at the nearby *taverna*. The food was excellent and he had ended his meal with several glasses of Greek wine.

By the following day, Nick had devised a plan as to how he would break down the walls that Alexis had so effectively built. He arranged for a bouquet of exotic flowers to be delivered to Alexis at her apartment along with a bottle of the best Greek wine he could find. Because of the warmer climate in Crete, Nick was able to choose from a wide variety of flora and had the florist fill a decorative hatbox with roses, orchids, chrysanthemums, and imported greens.

Nick wrote Alexis a short letter to be delivered with the flowers and wine. He was much better at expressing himself in writing than he was verbally. It gave him time to think about what he wanted to say and how he wanted to say it. His letter read:

> Dear Alexis:
> There is a good looking, brilliant architect who would like to meet with you. He thinks you are the most beautiful woman he has ever laid eyes on and will not rest until he has had a chance to talk to you. He realizes that he is very undeserving of your

charm and beauty, but wondered if you would grace him with your magnificent presence for only a short while.

Please call me so that I can take this man out of his misery. Phone number where I am staying: +3 (081) 811731

Very truly yours,
Nick

Nick had given the delivery boy an extra twenty bucks to put a rush on Alexis's order ensuring that she'd get the flowers, wine and letter that afternoon. With luck, she'd call him before evening. He decided to stay in his room and wait for Alexis to call. Confident that he was doing the right thing, Nick passed the time by going over some work that he had brought with him.

When Nick's phone rang at 2:00, he self-confidently picked it up. Who else could it be but Alexis? "This is Nick."

"Nick, this is Alexis." Her voice did not hold the warmth Nick had anticipated.

"I was hoping you'd call."

"Did you really think that you could change my mind with some high-school boy approach?" Alexis sounded exasperated.

"Don't tell me that a high school boy would have sent you a beautiful flower arrangement like the one I did along with a bottle of the best Greek wine."

"And it's so typical of you to be arrogant enough to refer to yourself as brilliant *and* good looking in your letter!" Alexis said shrilly.

Nick held the phone away from his ear momentarily, then when it was safe to put the receiver against his ear again he said, "Alexis, please meet with me. I just want to talk to you like two adults."

"No way. I have a sailboat booked for this afternoon. I have to leave now if I'm going to make it."

"I'll take you to dinner then. Will you call me when you get back?" Nick asked hopefully.

"If I've cooled off enough by then." Although Alexis was still perturbed, she had softened slightly.

"Okay. I'll talk to you later." Nick hung up the phone.

Alexis had to admit, the flowers *were* beautiful. And although the note was a bit much, it was thoughtful of Nick to have taken the time to write it in the first place. *I want to hate him. I don't want to give him a chance to make things up to me. I don't want to think about my mom having any other man in her life besides my father.*

Alexis realized she was being incredibly stubborn about the whole situation. Nick had snubbed her from the start at their first meeting. Now that Alexis had something that *Nick* wanted, meaning a chance to get to know his father through Diana, he wasn't letting up. The man was obviously obsessed with the past and anything that had to do with the father he never knew.

Alexis had traveled to Greece several times with her father and brother. Diana had declined making these the trips, choosing instead to stay behind with Lela. André had family that still lived in Athens, and Alexis felt fortunate to have had the opportunity to meet them.

On one of their trips, the three of them had taken a 10-day excursion sailing from one island to another. There are over 200 islands in the Greek Isles, Crete is the largest and southernmost island. It had been a fabulous trip and Alexis cherished the memories of that wonderful time spent with her father and brother.

Alexis gathered her canvas bag with the items she thought she would need for her afternoon sailboat excursion. It was a beautiful, warm sunny day, perfect for sailing in the tepid blue waters of the Mediterranean.

Making her way down to the docks, Alexis was unaware that she was being watched. She looked like a Grecian goddess in a white full-piece bathing suit and wrap around skirt. On her feet, she wore a pair of sandals that were secured by a strap that crisscrossed over the front of her foot. Her straight, glossy dark hair was pulled back in a long ponytail, and she had on a pair of dark sunglasses. Nick was overwhelmed with how absolutely stunning she looked.

When Alexis reached the waiting sailboat, the friendly owner with whom she had arranged the excursion greeted her. He eagerly helped her onto the boat and assisted her in getting comfortable before launching out to sea.

Nick waited until the sailboat was a good ways out before starting the engine of the small motor boat he had rented. He didn't want Alexis to know he was following her. What else was he supposed to do all day? Okay, so there was the museum and open air market, but Alexis was much more interesting and beautiful to look at.

The sailboat clipped along at a fairly fast pace. Wind and salt water spray whipped at Alexis's face. She breathed deeply of the clean sea air. *This is what heaven must be like.* With a catch in her throat, she thought of her dad and wondered if he could see her now.

With the mandatory life vest over her bathing suit, Alexis sat near the guardrail of the sailboat and looked over the edge at the fast moving water and the wake the boat left behind. The owner of the boat expertly maneuvered the sails with the help of one other crewmember.

Suddenly, and without any prior warning, a huge gust of wind caught hold of the main sail. In a flurry of activity, the two men fought desperately to keep the sailboat upright. Before she realized what was happening, Alexis was thrown from the boat into the deep blue waters of the Mediterranean along with the crew.

Panic-stricken, Alexis dazedly looked around her. The choppy waters made it almost impossible for her see the two men who had been sailing the boat. Her head throbbed where she had struck it on her way over the railing of the sailboat.

Slowly, as if she were treading through gelatin, Alexis made her way over to the two men. Just as she was about to reach them, she heard the sound of a motorboat. Help was on its way!

"Grab my hand and get in!" Nick yelled over the sound of the engine to Alexis.

"Nick! What…?" Alexis was stunned.

"Hurry, get in." Nick held out his hand and helped Alexis into the boat.

"I'm so glad to see you! We have to get the others." Alexis looked anxiously out over the water. Once inside the boat, she could see that one of the men was unconscious and the other man was floating next to him helping to keep his head above water.

"I'm going to pull the boat closer to them, then I'll need you to take the wheel so I can get the unconscious guy into the boat first." Nick didn't wait for a reply. He slowly directed the boat the few feet to where the men were.

Alexis took the wheel as Nick helped to get the unconscious man into the boat and then assisted the other. Alexis drove the boat back to the docks as Nick administered CPR to the unconscious man, who was barely breathing. By the time Alexis pulled the boat in to the dock, the man was breathing on his own but was weak and worn out for his ordeal. He had a huge lump forming on his head from where the boom had knocked him overboard.

Both of the men were extremely grateful to Nick for helping them. Nick made sure that they would be taken care of before leaving them at the dock. Turning to Alexis, he asked, "Want me to walk you home?"

Alexis felt her face grow hot with humiliation. She felt that she owed him her life, in a way, or at least her gratitude. "Sure, thanks."

Nick took Alexis's hand in his. "You're freezing. Here put this on." He took off his windbreaker and placed it over her shoulders.

"Thanks," Alexis said through chattering teeth.

"I'll draw a hot bath for you when we get to your apartment."

Even in her misery, Alexis thought, *why does he have to be so wonderful?*

Moments later, Alexis was in her bedroom at the apartment stripping off her wet bathing suit. Then, wrapped in a white terrycloth robe, she went into the bathroom where Nick was sitting on the edge of the bathtub pouring bubble bath into the stream of hot water coming from the faucet.

"While you're taking your bath, I'll go into town and get some food for dinner. Do you think you'll be okay for about forty-five minutes while I'm gone?"

"Yes, thanks." Alexis smiled gratefully at Nick whose handsome features were etched with concern.

Kissing her forehead, Nick left the bathroom, closing the door behind him. Alexis removed her robe and stepped into the warm soothing water. She didn't think she'd want to get near water ever again in her life after today, but the bubbles were tempting and sweet smelling and they helped to calm her jangled nerves.

Nearly forty minutes later, Nick returned loaded down with bags of food. He had taken a cab into town and generously tipped the driver for taking him from one store to another and waiting while he made his purchases. Nick busily went about preparing a feast for himself and Alexis. Fresh lamb was cubed and skewered between chunks of green peppers and onions. Once the shish kabob was under the broiler, Nick made a salad of fresh greens and local vegetables.

When Alexis came out of her bedroom shortly after Nick's return, she was pleasantly surprised. A large, round candle had been placed on the kitchen counter spreading a soft glow over the room. A bouquet of fresh flowers had been artfully arranged in a shallow, decorative dish and two wineglasses had been set out and filled with white wine. The savory smell of green peppers and onions cooking filled the air.

Nick had been so busy preparing the food that he hadn't heard Alexis enter the kitchen.

"I have one question. Do you do laundry?" Alexis asked, placing one hand on her cocked hip, observing Nick curiously.

Nick jerked his head around to see Alexis posed in the kitchen with her hand on her slender, shapely hip. She was wearing a light blue dress that fell off of her shoulders seductively. The skirt of the dress fell mid-thigh, showing off her stunning legs. Her dark hair was flowing softly over her bare shoulders and her face looked more relaxed than it had earlier.

"I'll do anything you want as long as you stand there looking at me like that." Nick said, catching Alexis off guard.

"Like what?" Alexis took her hand off her hip and crossed her arms defensively in front of her.

"Never mind. Have a glass of wine while I serve the food." Nick waved his hand towards the wineglasses.

Alexis sat down at the counter and slowly sipped her wine. She found herself unable to keep her eyes off of Nick. Thankfully, his back was turned to her as he busily arranged the food on the plates. Even in the kitchen, she noted, Nick had an air of authority and of someone who demanded excellence. There was also an aura of loneliness about him.

"How come you're not married?" Alexis surprised herself by asking this question out loud.

"How come *you* aren't?" Nick asked, not turning around.

"I asked you first." Alexis said playfully.

"No time. I've been so busy building my business that getting married would have been unfair to a woman. I would never have been able to give a wife the attention that she deserves."

"That's a good reason." Alexis was pleased to hear that Nick placed marriage in such high esteem.

"Your turn," Nick looked over his shoulder at Alexis expecting her to answer the same question she had posed to him.

"Same reason. I've been busy and a relationship would have suffered at my hands. I'm not very domesticated, thanks to my father," Alexis said without apology.

Plates in hand, Nick turned with easy grace and set the food on the counter. Before sitting down next to Alexis, he placed a loaf of freshly baked Greek bread on a cutting board and sliced several pieces for them to eat with their meal.

"This is wonderful. I don't know how to thank you Nick," Alexis said after finishing her first bite of food.

"I figured you'd need a nice quiet night after what happened today."

Alexis nodded her head in agreement. "That was the first time I've ever been in a situation like that, and I hope to never be again."

"I'm glad I happened to be nearby. Who knows how long you would have waited in the water before someone realized what had happened."

Alexis paused, her fork mid air. "How is it that you were there?"

"Well, when you said you were going sailing, I decided that it was a beautiful day to be on the water and rented a motorboat. I found myself following the sailboat you were on." Nick looked down, embarrassed that he'd admitted the truth to her.

"I never thought I'd live to see the day when Nick Agorinos was ashamed of something he'd done." Alexis said.

"Hey, I'm glad I was there to save you." Nick's momentary embarrassment was completely gone now.

"Me too. Under any other circumstance I'd have been furious with you for following me. I have to admit, it seems as though fate played a hand in today's events."

Leaning slightly forward towards Alexis, Nick said, "Fate seems to be playing a hand in our *lives*, Alexis—yours and mine." His dark eyes earnestly sought her green ones.

"Nick, please don't get serious with me." Alexis was confused by her unexpected response to him.

"You're the first woman I've ever known that I felt I could fall in love with, Alexis."

"You don't know me well enough to say that." Her mind was reeling with confusion.

"I know right here," Nick pointed to his heart, "that you're the one."

"I happen to like my life just the way it is. I like being able to do what I want whenever I want. I'm no good at having a relationship." Alexis let out a sigh of annoyance. She felt unwilling to face him, yet unable to turn away.

"We don't have to have a relationship then. How about if we start out as friends and business associates? We've got the next year to work on the mall together and get to know one another better." Nick struggled to maintain an even tone. The last thing he wanted to do was frighten her away.

Alexis had no intention of giving in to him. She didn't have time to be distracted by love and romance. However there was an undeniable attraction between them. A rage of emotions warred within her. With some difficulty, Alexis walked away from Nick and opened the sliding door that led onto the outdoor deck.

The sun was setting behind the sea, and there was the sound of waves lapping gently against the shore. Alexis stood still, listening to the melody of the descending nightfall all around her.

Nick came up behind her and took her hands in his own. "Close your eyes, Alexis."

A ripple of awareness shot through her as Alexis did as she was told. Slowly, gently, Nick kissed the back of her neck making a searing trail down one shoulder then across her back to the other shoulder. When he reached the other side of her neck, Alexis let out a moan of desire. "Nick, please…"

"Please…what?" Nick's voice was a tender whisper in her ear. He noticed that her eyes were still closed.

"Please don't make me fall in love with you." It was a soft, pleading request.

"Why not? Why shouldn't we fall in love?" Nick was still standing behind Alexis holding her hands in his own as he encircled her waist.

"Because I don't feel right about it. Doesn't it seem strange to you that your father and my mother were once in love? I loved my own father very much. When my mother's parents died, she became emotionally unreachable. If it weren't for my father I wouldn't be who I am today." Alexis had grown rigid in Nick's arms.

"Your father did a fine job raising you Alexis. You're a beautiful and intelligent woman. I believe that higher forces are at work here though." Nick nuzzled his face into her neck, refusing to let go of the feeling they'd shared just a moment ago.

"I can't believe that a logical man like you believes in 'higher forces.'"

Nick removed his arms from around her waist and gently turned Alexis towards him. "Maybe *we're* getting the chance that *they* never had, Alexis. Maybe there's a reason that we found one another and are attracted to each other. You aren't betraying the memory of your father by falling in love with me. I'd like to believe that I'm the kind of guy he'd want you to be with."

Alexis swayed gently at the truth of his words. Yes, it was true. Nick was exactly the kind of guy that her father would have approved of. Nick was intelligent, ambitious, and hard-working, just as André had been.

Lightly, Nick stroked her cheek. "I already know that I love you, Alexis. I'm sorry if that scares you. I'm willing to wait for you to fall in love with me too."

Alexis moved towards Nick, compelled involuntarily by her own passion. She pressed her lips to his in a slow caressing kiss.

Placing his hands on her face, Nick held her lips to his own drinking in her sweetness. Their bodies swayed gently to a shared rhythm.

The shrill ringing of the telephone rudely jolted Nick and Alexis back to reality.

Breathlessly, as though she had been caught doing something forbidden, Alexis hurried over to answer the phone. "Hello?"

"Alex, it's Andrew. Listen, you don't need to come home, but I thought you should know that Mom's in the hospital."

"What?" Alexis cried out in alarm. "Why?"

"They think she may have had a stroke. She lost her balance earlier today and hit her head pretty hard. They've run some more tests on her." Andrew said uneasily.

"Why didn't you call me sooner?" Alexis asked, forgetting her own frightening ordeal that same afternoon.

"I figured you were out at the beach or something, and I didn't want to ruin your day."

Realizing she'd practically been drowning in the sea that very afternoon, Alexis simply said, "Oh, yeah, I was at the beach." No need to alarm Andrew twice in one day. She was safe and sound now.

"Did Nick make it there okay?"

"He's here with me now. He made dinner for me and we were just…talking."

"Right. Well, I know you don't like anyone telling you what to do, but I think you should give him a chance. He seems like a decent guy, Alexis."

"I have to admit, I was ready to come home and strangle you at first, but things will work out okay. I'll probably come home tomorrow if I can book a flight."

"It's up to you. Call me and let me know."

Alexis hung up the phone and turned to look at Nick. "My mom is in the hospital. The doctors think she may have had a stroke."

Nick went over to where she was still standing by the phone and rested a reassuring hand on her waist. "If you want to, we can fly back home tonight."

"It was foolish of me to come all the way out here in the first place. I knew my mother's condition had become worse, but I needed to get away."

"I'm sorry I'm the reason you ran. I never meant to spring everything on you like that. The letters, the keepsakes, I knew that day at Dr. William's office, when your mother thought I was my dad, that she was the Diana in the letters. I wanted to wait for the perfect moment to share them with you."

"There may never have been a good time to show me that stuff, Nick. I overreacted. You came all this way for nothing."

"I wanted to explain things to you in more detail. You wouldn't give me a chance that night at my house."

Alexis needed to think, put emotion aside. "When I was growing up, it was very difficult having a mom who was mentally incapacitated. Whenever I'd invite a friend over after school, my mother would do or say embarrassing things. The next day at school was pure hell because whomever I'd had over the day before was telling everyone what a freak my mom was. You know how cruel kids can be. I became a loner."

"I didn't have to deal with my mom becoming ill until recently." Nick rubbed his hand down Alexis's arm.

"I was the proverbial poor little rich girl. My father had money and I had an aunt who looked after me. I didn't get any sympathy from anyone. I learned that I didn't need it. All I needed was to get good grades in school and learn my father's business. I was happiest when I was submersed in a project with him. Nothing else mattered."

"You never took the time to think about whether or not you were truly happy, did you?"

Alexis shook her head. "I still don't think about it much. I'm 30 years old and have never had a serious relationship with anyone. I don't know how to."

"Having a mentally ill member of the family is very time consuming. Even when you're not with them, you're thinking about them and their welfare. We're both fortunate enough to have someone who can help us look after our mothers." Nick's low, soft voice had a welcome, calming effect.

Alexis walked lazily over to the sliding door. The sun had made its complete descent behind the water. In its place, the moon and a million stars illuminated the night sky. "It's so beautiful here. I wonder what it must have been like to live here."

"When my mom and I left, Greece was still recovering from the war. America was the place to be if you wanted a better way of life."

"Better as in modern, fast and rude? Isn't that what our lives have become?" Her voice was calm, but with no hint of warmth or tenderness.

She was still looking out over the water when he took his place behind her. The touch of his hand on her shoulder was unbearably tender. "Walk with me along the beach," he whispered, his voice melting her, turning her insides to liquid.

Alexis had spent a lifetime resisting temptation. Other men had tried to break through the emotional barrier she'd so effectively built around her. All had failed.

Maybe she was getting tired of fighting, but Nick was getting to her.

They walked outside, the night air balmy and fragrant. A lover's moon hung in the night sky and the sea rolled up the sandy beach in gentle waves. In some remote part of his brain, Nick knew he shouldn't pull Alexis towards him, but he did, and he could hear her sharp intake of breath from his sudden action. Cupping her chin, he turned her face to his. Something sparked in her eyes, and he covered her mouth with his own before she could speak.

The beach was deserted, the only light provided by the moon created wispy shadows. The noise of the surf drowned out the thudding of her heart as she felt a slender, delicate thread of intimacy begin to form between them. His appeal was devastating. Alexis found herself drowning in the sweetly intoxicating nearness of him.

Nick rubbed her bare shoulders with hands that shook with barely controlled desire. He brought them down the length of her body, feeling the curve of her waist, the flair of her hips where he let his hands rest. Nick pulled Alexis firmly against his torso as an upward surge of heat shot through him, her moan of desire kindling an already blazing fire within him. The air around them was charged with sensual energy.

"Let me stay the night with you, Alexis," he begged, his lips never leaving hers.

"Nick, you don't understand," she pulled back to stare at him with longing.

"I understand that fate brought us together. I know it without a doubt, Alexis."

Alexis stood staring quietly at him, "Nick, I've…"

"What is it? What's wrong?" He was peering at her intently.

Alexis shook her head and ran from him, towards the deck and through the sliding doors. In the kitchen, she leaned one hand on the counter to catch her breath, and gain control of her scattered thoughts. What was wrong with her? She was filled with an unbearable desire for Nick, yet she couldn't allow herself to fulfill her aching need. Not yet.

Nick came up behind her, wanting to touch her, but afraid to. Instead, he ran a shaking hand through his hair.

"I'm sorry, Nick."

"No, I'm sorry. I shouldn't have come on to you like that. It's just that, well, we're both adults, and the night was romantic, and it just seemed like the natural thing to do."

"Maybe it is for most people, when they know what the hell they're doing." There, she'd said it. Her back was still turned to him, but she'd admitted the truth. She felt a shudder of humiliation.

"When they know what they're doing? What the..." Nick paused mid-sentence, as awareness broke across his face. He did not trust himself to speak any further.

Alexis felt her embarrassment turn to annoyance as she spun around to face him. "Thirty-year-old, worldly, Alexis Stephanos is still a virgin." There, she'd said it.

Nick held his palms outward to stop Alexis. "Look, I'm sorry. I had no idea. I just figured, well, you know..."

"You figured wrong. In fact, it seems that you've formed a lot of opinions about me, and you don't even know me."

"You're right." Nick looked down at his feet. He was having trouble looking directly at her. Man, he was really blowing his chances with her. He wasn't sure if he had any left. Silence loomed between them for several minutes. Finally, Nick asked, "Did you want to leave for home tomorrow to be with your mother?"

Alexis nodded her head. "Yes," she said softly, her eyes seeking his, but he refused to look at her. Instead, he was looking out the window.

"I'll make the arrangements and phone you. I'll book the earliest possible flight."

"Okay." She realized that their night was coming to an unhappy close, and she felt helpless to do anything about it. "Nick…"

He walked over to Alexis and put his arms around her. Kissing her forehead, he said, "I'm going to call a cab. We both should get some sleep tonight, we have a long trip home tomorrow."

Nick gently let go of Alexis and went over to use the phone. After hanging up, he turned to her. "I would never hurt you, Alexis. I'm sorry about the way tonight turned out. I'll make it up to you. We'll build the most beautiful, successful mall in Chicago."

Alexis visibly relaxed. "Thanks, Nick."

The tension between them eased and they talked about insignificant things while waiting for the cab to arrive.

"I'll see you tomorrow," Nick looked warmly into her eyes before leaving.

Alexis blew out the candle that was still burning on the kitchen counter. She went into her bedroom, and without undressing fell onto her bed. What was wrong with her? When was she going to open up and let someone in emotionally, physically? Why did everything have to be so difficult? She cried herself to sleep. It had been one really terrible day.

Son of a bitch! Nick thought to himself as he stripped down to his underwear and got into bed. Who would have guessed that a hot little number—no, a thirty-year old, hot little number like Alexis was still a virgin? Especially having lived through the "anything goes", "if it feels good, do it", attitude of the sixties! Nick hadn't thought there were any virgins left over the age of 16.

He'd blown it again with her. He'd assumed things about her that were totally incorrect. He didn't deserve to be within one inch of a woman of her caliber. Yet he had been tonight. His body stirred with desire as he remembered kissing her on the beach.

How could he make it up to her? They would work on the mall together, for one thing. And, he was going home with her so that she could be with her mother. That should count for something.

Nick fell asleep that night thinking of ways to win Alexis Stephanos over to his heart, and eventually, into his bed.

CHAPTER TWENTY-SIX

Nick had been able to get a flight leaving the Heraklion airport at 2:30 p.m. and landing at Chicago's O'Hare airport at 6:45 a.m. the next morning. He'd called Alexis to let her know the travel plans.

"Nick, please come by and have lunch with me. I need to talk to you. We can spend the morning together."

It didn't take much prodding. "Sure, I'll see you around 10:00. I'll pack and check out, and we can leave for the airport from your place."

"Okay." She was ready to face him again. Ready to define their relationship.

On the cab ride over, Nick felt his palms get sweaty. What was he supposed to say to her? Nothing, he decided. He would act normal as though everything was fine. Maybe she would initiate a conversation about last night, then he could just answer her questions, preferably with a yes or no.

Alexis opened the door wearing a full-piece bathing suit, cut down to her belly button and accentuating the swell of her breasts, causing Nick another round of physically painful memories. She was making it hard for him to be a nice guy.

"Planning on going for a swim?" He asked, setting his luggage down in the foyer.

"I thought we'd have a picnic near the ocean before leaving for the airport."

"Sounds like a great idea. Might as well enjoy Paradise for one more day. I'll change into my swimming shorts." Nick unzipped one of his suitcases and pulled out a pair of cut-off Levi's. Several moments later, he emerged from the bathroom.

Alexis was waiting outside on the deck for him. Behind her sunglasses, she took in his lean, beautifully proportioned body, as he joined her. The cut-off, denim shorts fell slightly above mid-thigh revealing strong, muscled legs. A patch of dark hair covered his belly button, leading downward below the snap of his shorts. His chest was smooth, with a light sprinkling of hair, and his shoulders were broad and athletic looking. She handed him the blanket, picked up the picnic basked, and they walked together silently out to the warm, white sand.

The beach was deserted, as it had been the night before. "Looks like we have the place to ourselves." Alexis said. She noticed that Nick was unusually quiet. "I guess this spot is fine. Will you help me spread out the blanket?"

Together, they opened the blanket and set the picnic basket on top of it. Alexis opened the top and took out suntan lotion and a Frisbee.

"Want some lotion?" She held up the bottle of Coppertone.

"Sure," he reached to take the bottle from her, but she held on to it.

"I'll rub it on for you."

He turned his back to Alexis and closed his eyes, enjoying the sensation of the lotion being smoothed over his skin. She covered his back, shoulders and neck, then put some lotion on her own legs and arms. "Will you get my back for me?"

"Sure," he replied, trying not to think of his task at hand as he spread the lotion over her bare, satiny skin. He needed a distraction or he was going to be all over her in a minute. "Let's play Frisbee." He grabbed the disc and shot up, running nearer to the water.

Alexis joined him, the warm, wet sand squished between her toes as she ran to catch the Frisbee he had thrown towards her. After a while, Nick started to show off, throwing it between his legs, and catching it from behind his back.

"Show off!" Alexis laughed.

Nick ran up to her, grabbed her around the waist, wrestled her playfully to the sand. "You're the show off. I can hardly think straight with you in that damn bathing suit. You're lucky we made it out to the beach at all."

He tickled her until she was begging him to stop. They rolled in the sand, laughing. Then, Alexis was reaching for him, pulling him towards her. His tongue traced her lips, and she shivered with delight. Greedily, he kissed her neck, and followed the open neckline of her swimsuit. She arched her back demanding more. His hand burned a path down her abdomen to her thigh.

Alexis felt drugged by his kisses. She was shocked by her response to this man. Nick was running his thumb up and down her inner thigh and she was drawn to a height of passion she had never before experienced.

A dog barking in the not-so-far distance caused Nick and Alexis to pull apart and look up. Running towards them was a large, black Labrador. He scooped the Frisbee up in his mouth and headed towards his master.

"Thor, no!" It was a man in his late fifties. He took the Frisbee from his dog and handed it to Nick. "I apologize. He likes to play." The man shrugged his shoulders and continued walking. "Thor, come!"

Nick and Alexis were standing, covered in sand. Alexis looked over at Nick, then down at herself. "Look at us," she said, wide-eyed, and took off running into the waves, Nick following close behind.

One of these days, they'd get to finish what they'd started.

"You're in an airplane on your way home. What more can you do?" Nick asked rhetorically.

Tears of frustration welled up in Alexis's eyes. "Nothing except get home as quickly as I can. Can't this plane go any faster?"

Taking her hand in his, Nick rubbed the back of it with his thumb. "Try and get some sleep. You'll need to be fresh when you get home. You won't be any good to your mom if you're tired and cranky."

"I'm not cranky!" Alexis said under her breath.

"Shhh." Nick closed his eyes hoping his action would encourage Alexis to do the same. "Try and get some sleep."

Alexis fluffed the small pillow that the stewardess had given her and placed it on Nick's shoulder. Putting her head on the pillow she let out a frustrated sigh then closed her eyes. "By the way, Nick, I had fun this morning," she said, eyes still closed.

Nick took her hand again and resumed rubbing the back of it gently with his thumb; in a matter of minutes, Alexis was fast asleep.

A dizzying current raced through Nick. Within the span of one week, he had found Diana and met the woman he wanted to marry. He knew it was going to take some time for Alexis to feel the same way about him, but after today, he knew that it was only a matter of time.

How could he have been such an idiot at their first meeting? Nick wished he had a chance to relive that day; he would have played his part much differently. In retrospect, he realized that he was very proud of Alexis. She hadn't put up with his nonsense for one minute. She was a tough number, all right, with a soft heart. Nick smiled to himself as he drifted off to sleep, his cheek resting against Alexis's head.

By the time Nick and Alexis had gathered their luggage and retrieved their cars from long-term parking, it was almost 7:30 in the morning.

"I'm not sure where to go first, so let's go to my mom's house. Andrew may have stayed there with my aunt Lela." Alexis suggested to Nick who then followed her in his own car.

Alexis was only mildly surprised when Andrew sleepily answered the door. He perked up immediately upon seeing his sister. "Alex, I'm so glad you're home!"

"How is she?" Alexis asked, referring to her mother.

"The same. I told the hospital to notify Dr. Williams and he's been in to see her."

"Good." Alexis said, relieved.

Andrew turned to Nick, "Good to see you again."

Nick smiled and returned Andrew's warm welcome. "Good to see you, too. I'm sorry to hear about your mom. I hope everything's going to be okay."

"Me too." Andrew said. "Visiting hours start at 9:00. Are either of you hungry?"

Alexis shook her head. "We ate and slept on the plane."

"Looks like you two were able to work a few things out." Andrew smiled approvingly, noticing how relaxed they each seemed. "I'll wake aunt Lela and let her know you're here so she can get ready and come with us. I'll be down in ten minutes after I wash up." Andrew headed for the staircase.

"Okay," Alexis said to Andrew as he hurried up the stairs. Turning to Nick, she said, "Let's go into the kitchen and make some coffee while we wait for them."

By 10:00, Andrew, Lela, Nick, and Alexis were gathered around Diana's hospital bed. Fortunately, Diana had been placed in a private room and the four visitors didn't have to be concerned about disturbing

another patient. She was sitting up in bed when they arrived. A large bandage covered the right side of her forehead.

"Alexis, you shouldn't have come all the way home just because of me."

Diana pulled Alexis close in a hug. She had been seated on the bed next to her mother.

"Nonsense, I can always go back to Greece any time I want. It's much more important for me to be here for you now." Alexis responded, waving away her mother's concern.

Diana had the mandatory IV providing continual fluids through a vein in her right hand. There was a portable ECG machine nearby which had previously been monitoring Diana's heart rate and rhythm.

"Well, what do we have here? No one told me there was a party going on!"

Dr. Williams said as he entered the room. Recognizing Alexis he said, "I heard you were going to fly back home from Greece, you sure didn't waste any time."

"When my brother called me I just had to come home right away." Then, calling his attention to Nick, she said, "Nick Agorinos is a friend of the family. You treat his mother, also."

Dr. Williams shook Nick's hand. "Yes, I do. Hello, Nick."

"So, do you know anything more about my mother's condition?"

"Yes. Her initial CAT scan, the one I intended to review with you at your mother's follow-up visit, indicates some areas of damage on the right side of the brain."

"Sounds serious." Andrew said.

"Essentially, a stroke is an injury to the nervous system which controls all bodily functions. When the blood vessels fail to supply an adequate amount of blood to the brain, an injury can occur."

"Is that why she passed out?" Alexis asked.

"You mother suffered a TIA, which is a small stroke. No further injury was evident on yesterday's CAT scan. Among other symptoms, a sign of a stroke can be unexplained dizziness or unsteadiness, which is what happened to your mom." Dr. Williams said, resting a comforting hand on Diana's shoulder.

"How long do you think she's been suffering from this condition?" Alexis couldn't keep the note of guilt from her voice. She felt ashamed at not having taken her mother to a doctor sooner.

"It's hard to tell. Some people suffer minor strokes for years without any prolonged or debilitating side effects." Dr. Williams explained. "Your mother is not in a high risk category because she isn't overweight and she doesn't smoke. I'd say that she could go on for many years experiencing only minor TIA's. Most of the damage has taken place on the right side of the brain, in the area that affects spatial orientation, which would account for her time disorientation and altered attention span."

"I think I understand. That's why she reverts to the past." Alexis said thoughtfully. "How can we prevent her from falling when she gets a dizzy spell in the future?"

"You can't. However, I am going to start her on medication that will improve her blood flow and hopefully prevent future TIA's. You should be able to take your mother home tomorrow."

"I can't wait to go home," Diana said, relieved. She was incredibly alert and aware of her surroundings.

"I'll fill out the necessary paper work for your release. You'll do fine, Diana. You're surrounded by people that love you," Dr. Williams said, before leaving the room to finish his rounds.

"They'll be serving lunch soon," Lela said to Diana, whose expression was one of pained tolerance.

"Why don't you kids go about your business. I'll stay here. You can come and visit your mother again tonight." Lela said, addressing Andrew and Alexis.

"Okay. I have a couple of appointments. I'll be back around 5:00, then." Andrew said, feeling strangely comforted now that he knew what they were dealing with where his mother was concerned.

"We have work to do, too. Alexis and I have a busy year ahead of us," Nick spoke to all, but his eyes were on Alexis.

Alexis felt herself blush under his intense gaze.

Andrew kissed his aunt and his mother good-bye, then waved to Nick and Alexis as he left.

"I'll come back at 5:00, too." Alexis said to her mother and aunt Lela. "Nick and I will be at my office if you need to get a hold of me before then." As she bent to kiss her mother good-bye, Diana stopped her.

"Whatever happened in the past should be forgiven. I loved Nikoli very much," she felt Alexis stiffen slightly, "but I also loved your father. I have two beautiful, intelligent children because of him."

Alexis wasn't used to having an intense, coherent conversation with her mother. She wasn't sure how she felt about it, especially now. "Is that all that matters? Or do you wish that you could have stayed in Greece with your parents and married Nikoli?"

Something flickered in Diana's eyes, a memory. "My life was spared when my parents sent me to America. For whatever reason, loyalty perhaps, Nikoli didn't come after me. That was his choice. I can't bring back the dead, Alexis, but I can see that your future is with Nick. Give him a chance. I know that your father would approve."

Her throat ached as a primitive grief overwhelmed her. She permitted herself the comfort of her mother's arms.

EPILOGUE

THE NEW MALL, NOVEMBER 1973

The Grand Opening of the new mall was in progress. Marshall Fields and Saks Fifth Avenue were anchored at either end of the mall with thirty other stores, boutiques, restaurants, and beauty shops throughout. The center of the mall boasted a large waterfall surrounded by comfortable seating where shoppers could relax.

An extensive advertising campaign had been underway for the past month to create an aura of excitement and fascination over the new mall. A shopper could purchase anything from lingerie to fine china among the many excellent establishments.

The outside area surrounding the mall was beautifully landscaped with bright flowers and sculpted shrubs. A large pond with a fountain graced the main driveway, and the main entrance to the mall had a valet booth for those who didn't want to be bothered with finding a parking space.

A two-story building of office suites had also been constructed and was connected to the mall by a glass-enclosed walkway. Alexis had moved her main headquarters for Stephanos Construction Company to the top floor. She and Nick stood looking out over the organized chaos below as car after car full of shoppers lined the parking lot.

"It's so beautiful, Nick. Everything is exactly how I pictured it. Maybe even better." Alexis said, turning to Nick to see the clear cut, handsome lines of his profile.

"You did a splendid job. Your father would be proud of you." Nick said, without turning his head away from the window.

"*We* did a splendid job. I couldn't have done it without you." Over the past year of working together, Nick had entirely unlocked her heart and soul.

"Just in time for the Christmas rush too. You'll have a great first few months of business." Nick turned his head to look at her. "So, what's next on your agenda?"

"Nothing for the next few months. I need a break from the hectic pace of this past year. How about you?" Alexis hadn't thought about what would happen to their relationship once the mall project ended. For the past year, it had been the glue that held them together. Nick had been very careful not to pressure Alexis emotionally, although he had succeeded several times to extract an ardent physical response from her.

"I have a few projects that my team has been working on over the past few months. I wanted to make sure that you had my undivided attention though, so I haven't gotten too wrapped up in anything yet," Nick replied. He secretly wished that Alexis would give him some sign that she wanted him in her life on a permanent basis. She was still so damn independent and hard to read.

"I appreciate the extra time you put in, Nick. It's made all the difference in the success of this project. You were right when you said I was biting off more than I could chew." Every day, Alexis's love for Nick had deepened and intensified, but she had yet to tell him.

"You would have been able to complete this project without me Alexis. You're an extremely determined woman and I'm proud to have been a part of your team." Nick turned towards her, and smiled. "I didn't even have to move any plug sockets around for you."

"No you sure didn't." Alexis stared at him with longing and walked over to stand in front of him. "Nick, I…" her voice trailed off and she looked away.

Nick put his hand out towards her face and tilted her chin towards him. "You what, Alexis? What did you want to say to me?" His dark eyes bore into her green ones, sensing her desire, and demanding an answer.

"I'm going to miss working with you. We've been together almost every day. I'm afraid that I've gotten more than a little attached to you." Alexis tried to stop the dizzying current that her words had created within. She'd practically told him that she loved him. If she didn't stop talking, she'd tell him and then it would all be over.

"Are you afraid to tell me that you love me, Alexis? Are you afraid I'll think you're weak if you do? How many times have I told you that I loved you over the past year only to have you make light of it?" Something in Nick's manner told her that she needed to make a decision. Soon.

"Nick…" Shoulders slumped in defeat, Alexis pulled away from Nick and walked back over to look out the window, not really taking in the scene below.

"I have to go now. I'll be in touch." Nick's voice was solemn and final. Without looking back, he left the office.

Alexis stood by the window, blinded by tears. How could she let him walk away like this? She felt her knees buckle slightly as she realized she couldn't. "Nick!" she cried out, running after him. Alexis didn't wait for the elevator, but instead took the flight of stairs to the first floor.

Nick was already headed for his car, which was parked in the private parking lot reserved for the office suite. He turned to look at Alexis as she came running over to him.

At that very moment, a Cessna flew by overhead dropping dozens of flowers over the parking lot where they were standing.

"What in the world?" Alexis cried out in astonishment. Although a large hot air balloon had been set on the roof of the main entrance to announce the event, she hadn't ordered a plane for the Grand Opening.

Walking over to one of the many flowers, she picked one up. They were roses. Dozens of them. And they each had a piece of paper attached to their stem with a golden thread. Puzzled, Alexis picked up one of the roses and unfolded the note. It read:

ALEXIS, WILL YOU MARRY ME?

Her heart pounded as she picked up one rose after another and unfolded the pieces of paper that were attached. Each note asked exactly the same thing.

"If you're looking for one with an answer in it, you won't find it. If it were that easy, I would have unfolded your heart a long time ago and found the answer I wanted."

Nick had walked over to Alexis and was standing over her where she was kneeling on the ground, roses strewn all around her.

Her body felt heavy and warm as she stood up to face him. Taking Nick into her arms, Alexis looked into his eyes. "Yes, Nick, I'll marry you. I love you more than I've ever loved anyone in my life."

"Say it again." Nick's body swayed into hers.

"I love you, Nick, I have for a long time, and I want to marry you." Alexis pulled this magnificent man to her in a renewed embrace. Then, pressing her open lips to his, she felt him succumb as his hand gently moved the length of her back.

With sudden realization, Alexis pulled away slightly to look at Nick. "You must have been planning that for quite a while."

Nick shrugged. "A couple of weeks. I couldn't just end the project without one final attempt."

"I'm sorry for being so difficult to get close to." Alexis said apologetically.

"Like a damn fortress," Nick agreed.

"You know what I'd like to do?" Alexis asked in a soft, seductive voice, kissing his chin.

"No, but I know what I'd like to do." Nick planted kisses on her lips between each word.

"Return to Greece, rent that apartment, and finish up where we left off last year." A shiver rippled through Alexis as the shock of his kisses ran through her body.

Nick was kissing her neck. "I don't think I can wait that long."

Pulling away entirely, Alexis took Nick's hand and led him back upstairs to her office. Locking the door, she pulled him down on the black leather sofa.

"I think we should have our own Grand Opening celebration." Alexis said, as she unbuttoned his shirt leaving a trail of kisses on his chest.

ABOUT THE AUTHOR

The second oldest of five children, Gina is the daughter of a home-maker, and a family physician. Growing up in the Detroit area, and working with her father, has provided Gina insight to many different cultures and customs, and her extensive travels across the United States lends depth to her writing. Her first novel, *Secrets That You Keep*, was published in September 2000. Gina lives in southeast Michigan with her four children.

Visit Gina's Website: *www.geocities.com/ginabeckers*

Printed in the United States
116578LV00003B/184/A